Hittin' Licks

D. M. Gaines

New Flavor
Books

W

Hittin' Licks

Copyediting and cover design by
Earvin Taze Watters
ezatcreations@yahoo.com
Revised January 2015

www.newflavorbooksandpublishingllc.com
New Flavor Books is an imprint of New Flavor Books & Publishing

New Flavor Books & Publishing LLC
P.O. Box 603323 Cleveland, Ohio 44103

Books by D M Gaines

Hood to Hood: A Cleveland Story
Hood to Hood 2: Spank's Revenge
Sexual Addiction: Director's Cut
All Flavors: A Book of Erotic Short Stories
Bisexual Bliss
Hitting' Licks
Murder or Justice
Deadly Surgeon

Dedication

This book is dedicated to all of the BC hustlers, the before crack hustlers, the hustlers from the early 80's, which was the era of the real hustlers.

Acknowledgements

I would like to give thanks to my best friend since childhood Darrin Fears. You are the only true friend that I have ever known. I would like to thank my daughter-n-law Beverly Johnson. Thank you for all of your help. And thanks to everyone out there, who supports me. May you all be blessed. I would like to give thanks to all of the following people. First and foremost I would like to thank my daughter Brittiny, without you this wouldn't have been possible, I love you. I would like to thank my mother Carol for giving me a gift that you always knew I had. I thank all the people from the Longwood and Garden Valley housing projects that I grew up with and who inspired this book. Also I would like to thank everyone at Victorville prison that were the first people to read my books and told me to keep doing my thing. That includes Bat, D-Ron, Twin, Poetic Gangsta and CJ. Thanks to all of y'all for your support. I hope that I can keep pushing out bangers. For everyone that has a dream, do not be afraid to pursue it. You are the only one that can come between you not making the dream a reality. All praise is due to Allah.
Sincerely Donny G

Chapter 1

1987 ...

Dirty Red, George and Rab were in a stolen car driving through downtown Cleveland. Their destination was the May Company department store. Red was driving and talking to two of his friends.

"Look its three mannequins with fur coats on, inside of the window. I'm going to run the car into the window and smash it then we are going to jump out of the car and take them coats."

The three of them were from the Garden Valley and Longwood housing projects in Cleveland, Ohio. They had started out boosting clothes. They would hit stores for their Polo, Izod and Hunt Club gear. They did that as a hustle and to stay fly. Dirty Red figured that they could make better money by hitting bigger licks. He just so happened was walking downtown one day and noticed the mannequins in the window of May Company department store wearing full length fur coats.

The fur coats were eight thousand dollars, he figured that he could at least sell them for three thousand apiece.

He told George and Rab about it and after explaining to them the amount of money that they could make off of the coats, they readily agreed. Dirty then went to Donny who he knew stole cars.

"Donny I need you to steal me a car, so that I can hit this lick!"

"What kind of car do you need?"

"It has got to be a big car I got to be able to run it through a window without it tearing up!"

"When do you need it?"

"I need it ASAP! I want to do this tonight."

"Okay, give me about an hour." Donny told him then he took off. Forty minutes later, Donny pulled back up in a 1977 Buick Park Avenue. Donny jumped out of the car cheesing, "Here you go."

"Donny you a down ass nigga, you always come through, how much do I owe you?"

"Just look out for me after you hit the lick, I ain't tripping." They gave each other dap.

"You know I got you my nigga, I'm out!" Red told Donny as he jumped into the car and pulled off, then Dirty headed to pick up George and Rab.

That was earlier in the day, now they were downtown about to hit the lick. It was about one in the morning and the traffic was light. Dirty turned down E. 4th and Prospect and headed towards Euclid Avenue. Once he got to Euclid, he made a left and drove a little ways until he was in front of May Company. He turned the lights out, and turned the car around until it was facing the front window of May Company.

"Hold on y'all! Brace yourselves!" Dirty told them as he hit the gas. The four barrel carburetor opened up and the car roared forward. Dirty was up to thirty miles per hour when the car jumped up onto the sidewalk and crashed into the front window of the store. The whole front end of the car was inside of the store.

Dirty quickly threw the car into reverse and backed the car up out of the store. Once the car was no longer blocking the entrance, all three of them jumped out of the car and ran into the store. Dirty had knocked two of the mannequins down. Him and George ran over to them and removed the fur coats, while Rab removed the one from the mannequin that was still standing.

They all ran out of the store and jumped back into the car. Dirty sped off, turning the headlights back on, only to find that only one was still working. They made it back to Garden Valley safely.

They parked the car in a parking lot, jumped out of it, and headed to Rab's house to stay the night. Dirty told them, "In the morning we are going to see Hobo, we should be able to get three grand apiece!"

Ÿ

The next day, Dirty Red, George and Rab walked through the projects sporting the full length fur coats, with the price tags still on them. It was the middle of the summer, with the temperature at eighty degrees. They walked up onto the weed strip. Everyone was looking at them like they were crazy.

"Y'all niggas are crazy as hell!" said one of the hustlers on the block named Bud.

"You know how we get down, but look I need you to give us a ride up to E. 118th and Union so that we can sell these!" Dirty told Bud.

"I leave this block and I'm going to lose out on money."

"We are going to take care of you. You won't be gone no longer than an hour."

"Enough said then, let's go." They all jumped into Bud's Chevy Nova and headed up to Hobo's store.

Hobo bought the furs. He gave them five thousand cash and four ounces in cocaine. Dirty gave George and Rab $2,400 each and told them that he would give them the other six hundred after he had his uncle sell the coke for him. He gave Bud two hundred dollars for giving them a ride. Bud took them back to the block and they headed their separate ways.

Dirty walked up the hill to his uncle Lofyette's apartment building. Loft as they called him, was standing outside of his building when Dirty walked up.

"What's up nephew?" he asked.

"I got four ounces of powder unc, how long will it take you to move them?"

"You want me to wholesale them or break them down?"

"If you break them down, how much can you make?"

"I probably can make three thousand off of each ounce if I stretch them."

"Damn! That's $12,000, how long will it take you to do that?"

"About two weeks, but I can give you something as the money comes in."

"Okay, you can keep four thousand for yourself." Dirty told him.

Ÿ

Tim, Mike and Ron were at the bus stop on E. 40th and Woodland. They each had pockets full of wheel bearings. They were preparing to do a bust & snatch.

They would wait for a car to stop at the red light, step off of the curb and use a bearing to smash in the passenger's side window. That would shock the driver and allow them to reach inside of the car and grab their purse off of the seat or their passport police radar off of the dashboard.

They would take turns doing bust & snatches, and then run through the projects to get away.

This day it was Mike's turn to pull a lick. He told the other two, "I ain't just hitting anybody. You got to wait for the right lick. All these white people ride through here on their way downtown to work. That is why the best times to do it is at seven in the morning and five in the evening. That is when people are going to and getting off of work."

"Okay, Mister I got it down to a science, let us see you work!" Tim said.

A bus pulled to a stop in front of them and they waved the bus driver off. The bus pulled off and the light changed to red stopping a line of traffic. Mike noticed that the third car had a middle aged white lady driving it. She was driving a newer model car, which to him indicated that she had money. Knowing that the lady was blocked in by traffic, Mike left the curb and jogged over to the woman's car. When the woman looked up he had his arm cocked back. He quickly threw the bearing, which smashed the car window and sent glass flying inside of the car. The lady screamed as she was hit by flying glass. Mike reached inside of the car and grabbed the woman's purse off of the passenger's seat. He then turned and took off running through the projects, with his partners in crime following. They knew that no one would attempt to chase them through the projects. They ran into the projects and entered an apartment building.

They ran up to the top floor where Mike emptied the contents of the purse out onto the floor. When Mike seen the wallet fall out, he grabbed it and started going through it. There was $145 in cash and two credit cards.

"Damn! There has got to be more than this!" Mike said as he picked through the rest of the things that he had dumped out on the floor. After he found nothing else, he put the contents back into the purse and flung the purse out of the hallway window.

"Shit!" Mike said angrily.

"What's wrong Mister I got it down to a science? Didn't get rich huh?" Tim asked him jokingly.

"Fuck you! Let's go downtown and try to use these credit cards."

"First things first, split that money up!" Ron said. Mike split the money up between them and they got $45 and some change apiece.

They walked downtown and entered a Chinese store. They picked out a couple of outfits then walked up to the counter. The

Chinese clerk rang up the outfits, and Mike handed him one of the credit cards to pay the bill. The clerk looked at the three boys suspiciously, then yelled out something in Chinese then another clerk came out of the back.

The first clerk whispered something into his ear then went into the back. The second clerk stood at the register watching the boys. The boys should have known that something was wrong from the amount of time that the clerk was spending in the back. After ten minutes, the clerk stepped from out of the back office waving his finger, "You steal credit card, no good, police are on the way here to get you, you go to jail!"

That was all the boys needed to hear. They took off running out of the store. They ran three blocks before they slowed down.

"We got to find a better way to make money!" Ron said.

"Yeah, we are doing shit that carries too much time to be only getting a little bit of paper!" Tim said.

"Yeah, we got to figure out a new way to make money!" Mike told them as they walked back to the projects.

Ÿ

Bruce, Keith and China Man were in the laundry room of a Green Court apartment building. They were running a train on the neighborhood runaway named Ramona. Bruce was fucking her while Keith and China Man stood waiting for their turn.

"Hurry up Bruce damn!" Keith said to him.

"Nigga! Don't rush me her pussy is good, I got to marinate in it!"

"Fuck that shit!" Keith said as he began unzipping his pants. He pulled his dick out and dropped down to his knees in front of Ramona. He tried to put his dick into Ramona's mouth, but she turned her head. Keith tried to turn her head back around, and then she yelled at Bruce, "Get up! Or I'm telling that y'all raped me!"

"Come on Mona stop tripping!" Bruce told her.

"Get up or I'm going to scream."

"Bruce, fuck that bitch!" Keith said as he got up and put his dick back in his pants.

"Nigga! You are always fucking shit up!" Bruce told Keith as he reluctantly got up off of Ramona.

"You a thirsty ass nigga, a nigga can't never get on fucking with you!" Bruce told Keith.

"Nigga! Stop tripping about that homeless bitch!"

"I ain't no bitch!" Ramona said as she pulled up her pants.

"Hoe! Shut the fuck up before I piss on you!" Ramona knew that Keith was crazy so she finished getting dressed and hurried up out of the laundry room.

"Fuck are we going to do now?" Bruce asked.

"Nigga, the Indians got a baseball game, let's go down there and hit some licks!" China Man said to them.

"If a nigga can't get no pussy, money is the next best thing, so let's go." Bruce said.

They walked to the bus stop and caught the bus downtown. They got off the bus on Public Square then walked down to the Cleveland Indians stadium. One by one they ducked down next to a person that was paying their admission and snuck into the stadium. Once inside they started casing out the vendors, looking for an easy lick.

Vendors had tables set up throughout the stadium advertising the things that they were selling. Underneath their table, they would usually keep their money box. The box would usually be a small tin or metal box that was easy to carry.

Bruce and his crew had hit the vendors for their money boxes plenty of times and had it down to an art. One of them would distract the vendor by pretending to want to buy some of their merchandise, while one of the other crew members would be on their knees crawling under the table in search of the money box.

Bruce, China Man and Keith saw a vendor of Indian descent. The vender was selling Cleveland Indians memorabilia.

"We can get him!" Bruce told the others.

"What's the plan?" asked China Man.

"I'm going to go and talk to the lame and get his attention. You get on your knees and crawl under the table. Keith you be the look out, let us know if any security guards are coming our way, y'all got it?" Keith and China Man shook their heads in agreement.

Bruce took off strolling over to the vendor's table. The vendor stood up when he noticed Bruce approaching. He put a smile on his face and in a deep West Indian accent asked, "How may I help you?"

"I would like to try on a size eight Pro Model hat."

"Step down here please, we have many styles to choose from." The vendor said indicating for Bruce to step down to the other end of the table where the hats were located. After seeing them walk to the other end of the table, China Man looked around making sure that the coast was clear. After making sure that it was all good he dropped down to his knees and began crawling. He crawled over to the table, reached his hand underneath it, and felt around looking for the strong box. He could not feel anything, so he stuck his head under the table. It was dark because the tablecloth that was on the table hung down to the floor on all sides of the table. China Man still could make out a silver box with metallic flakes in it. He reached out, grabbed the box, cuffed it, and then crawled from underneath the table.

Bruce was trying on a third hat, when he saw China Man walk away with the box. He ended the charade telling the vendor, "I just realized I got too many hats already. I'm sorry for taking up your time." He gave the vender the hat back and walked off.

Bruce, Keith and China Man headed towards the restroom. When they got inside, China Man opened the box and discovered that it was only sixty three dollars inside.

"Man, this is some bullshit!" Keith said.

"Fuck is we going to do with this?" asked China Man.

"Shit, let's just put it up and go and look for another lick!" Bruce said to them. They split the money up, getting twenty one dollars each. China Man threw the cash box into the trash and they walked out of the restroom. When they stepped outside of the bathroom, they heard someone yell, "That is them right there!" They all looked up and saw the Indian vendor flanked by two security guards, pointing in their direction. The security guards started heading their way.

"Go!" Bruce said. All three of them took off running through the stadium. They headed towards the exit, with the security guards hot on their heels. One of the security guards radioed in for back up. Bruce, Keith and China Man weaved through the crowd of people in the corridors bumping and even knocking people to the ground.

They were almost to the exit, when a big burly guard appeared in front of the turn style. He had a broad smile on his face, feeling that they would not be able to get past him. They saw the guard and came together like Voltron. They all ran directly at the guard at full force. They all hit the guard simultaneously, knocking him to the ground. They each then jumped the turn style and ran out into the parking lot. They ran up the ramp and over to the other side of the freeway, before they stopped to catch their breath.

"That shit was crazy!" Bruce said.

"We knocked that guard's big ass down!" China Man said laughing.

"His big ass had to go down, ain't no way I was going to jail over no damn $21!" Keith said as they headed back down the way.

"Man, we got to find some sweeter licks, because this shit is too risky!" Bruce said to the other two as they walked. They all agreed that they needed to find a better way to get money.

Chapter 2

A week had passed and Dirty went back to see his uncle Loft. Loft was sitting in a folding chair outside of his building when Dirty walked up.

"What's up unc?"

"Just sitting out here grinding, I got something for you, come on into the house." Loft got up and headed into the house with Dirty following behind him. They entered the house and Dirty's two little cousins Asia and Anna started to giggle and get excited.

"Hey cousin Dirty!" they both said in unison.

"Why are you two in the house, hot as it is outside?" Dirty asked them.

"We are on punishment!" Asia told him.

"What did y'all do?" Loft cut in, "Their fast asses been sneaking on the phone talking to boys late at night, when they are supposed to be sleep. Come on back to the bedroom." Dirty and Loft headed down the hall to Loft's bedroom. Loft entered the room first and told his girl Pat to cover up. Pat pulled the cover up over her naked bottom half, before Dirty entered the room.

Loft walked over to the dresser and pulled out the bottom drawer. He reached into it and pulled out a knot of money, then turned and tossed it to Dirty, "That's four grand, I should have you the other four by the end of next week."

"That's all good unc! I am about to go and buy me a car with this, the kid is tired of walking!"

"You know that you don't have any license, so you are going to have to put the car in somebody else's name."

"Are you going to do it for me unc?"

"What are you getting a car for Red? You aren't getting one to use it to do illegal shit is you?"

"No unc, I'm getting me a player's ride. I want a '79 Park Avenue or a Bonneville."

"Okay, look I know this white boy that has a lot on the west side. It's called Rick's trading post. It is a buy here pay here spot, meaning they finance you for the car themselves. Me and Rick are real cool, so I should be able to get you a deal."

"Let's shoot over there right quick and see what's up."

"Pat where are your car keys? I am about to shoot over to the west side right quick."

"They are on the living room table." Pat answered.

Dirty and Loft headed back up the hall, and as they walked past the living room table, Loft scooped up the car keys. On the way out of the door Dirty told his little cousins, "Y'all be good!"

They headed outside to the parking lot, and jumped into Pat's '78 Buick Regal.

Loft drove over to W. 61st and Lorain. There was the car lot Rick's trading post. It looked like a parking lot with a trailer home sitting in the middle of it, with cars parked all around it.

"This is a shabby ass looking lot unc! Do their cars work?"

"Yeah they work, he be going to dealer's auctions out in PA buying cars, then bringing them back and putting them on this lot. Pat got this car from here, and she done had it for over two years without having any major problems. Come on, let's go and see what he has on the lot."

They got out of the car and entered the fenced in lot. Loft headed to the trailer that had been converted into an office. When he entered, a huge country looking white boy with a beard that hung down to his huge pot belly, sat in a chair behind the desk. He looked up as Dirty and Loft entered. He smiled when he saw Loft.

"Well, hey there partner!" he said to Loft as he stood up to shake his hand.

"How are you doing Rick?" Loft asked

"Just trying to make a living, by golly." Rick Answered.

"Well, I brought you some business. This is my nephew Red and he is looking to buy a car."

"Hey there Red! What type of car are you looking for?"

"I'm trying to get me a Park Avenue or Bonneville."

"Well fella, you are in luck. I just happen to have a 1977 Park Avenue Limited Edition. It is gold, with a leather rag top and has a power sun roof. Also it is all power, would you like to see it?"

"Yeah!" Dirty told him.

They all headed out of the trailer, and Rick led them around the side of the trailer, where a gold Park Avenue sat gleaming. Dirty fell in love with the car at first sight. He walked over to the car and peered inside.

"Go ahead, get in and start her up, the keys are inside" Rick told Dirty. Dirty opened up the driver's side door and got in. He sunk into the gold crush velvet seat. The car still looked like new on the Inside. The keys were in the ignition. Dirty turned the key forward and started the car up. The car started right up and purred like a kitten. Rick walked over to the car and Dirty rolled down the power window

"Do you want to take her for a test drive?" he asked Dirty.

"Yeah!" Dirty answered.

"Okay, let me go and grab you a plate." Rick went back inside of the trailer and came back with a dealer's plate in his hand. He put the plate that was attached to a magnet on the back of the trunk.

"You go ahead and ride with him Loft, I got to stay here and look over the lot." Loft climbed into the passenger's seat and Dirty put the car in drive and pulled out of the lot driving up Lorain Ave.

As he was driving he reached over and turned the radio on. Loft reached over and cut the radio back off.

"Why did you do that unc?"

"Right now ain't no time to be listening to no music. Now is the time to be listening to the car. Listening to hear if anything sounds wrong, like knocking in the engine, clicking in the tire rod or whining in the transmission. Never go by how pretty a car looks Red. A car is just like a bitch, it could look good on the outside but be fucked up on the inside!"

"Point well taken unc!" They drove another four blocks in silence, and after not finding anything wrong with the car they headed back to the lot. When they pulled in, Rick was standing there beaming with pride. When they got out of the car he said, "Well, how do you like her? She is a beauty ain't she?"

"Yeah it's tight! How much do you want for it?"

"For you, I will take sixty five with half down, and payments of two fifty every two weeks."

"Okay, I'm going to give you thirty three hundred right now, but I am going to try to pay the car off within the next month."

"Lofyette, your nephew is my type of guy. Let's go into the trailer and get the paperwork done." They all stepped inside and Rick filled out the paperwork, putting the car in Loft's name. He issued them a temporary tag and they left the lot with Loft following Red. Dirty adjusted his seat using the electronic controls. He reclined the seat back as far as it would go, then put the tilt up on the steering wheel. He turned the radio to 93.1fm and cruised back over to the eastside.

Once they got to the Valley, Dirty pulled over and waved for Loft to pull along the side of him. Dirty yelled over to him, "I'm good unc, I'm about to go up to the school."

"Okay, you be careful and if you need me, you call me!" Loft told him then pulled off. Dirty rode up the hill to Rab's parking lot. He knew that Rab would not be in school. George was the only one out of the three of them that went to school regularly. School was George's stage. He went to school to perform. He would set new clothing trends, having the latest Guess and Swatch watches. The main thing was that all the girls at South High loved George, with his chipped tooth and all.

Ÿ

Dirty parked the car in the parking lot and got out leaving it running. He yelled up to Rab's apartment window, "A Rab! Yo Rabbit!" The curtain moved and Rab's dark face appeared in the window. He slid the window up, "Dirty what's up?"

"Come on nigga, we got to go up to the school to pick up George."

"Pick up George in what?"

"In my car nigga! Now come on before school lets out, I'm trying to floss." Rab shut the window and scrambled downstairs.

He stepped outside wearing guess jeans, a Cleveland Indians jersey with a matching Pro Model hat. On his feet was a pair of British Knights with snake skin around the heels.

Rab had come a long way from the days when he was referred to as dirty Rab. Coming from a poor family wasn't the bad part, because everyone in the projects was poor. Some was just poorer than others. It was Rab's appearance and smell that had earned him the name dirty Rab. Up until the age fourteen Rab had bad hygiene. He was always dirty, his hair was always nappy and he had a bad smell about him. A smell that originated in his home. People that did not frequently go to Rab's house would have to either hold their breath or their nose whenever they entered.

Rab would catch the blues from the older boys in the projects, but he would take it back out on the boys his age. Rab was very stocky. At twelve years old, he was built like he lifted weights daily. He was dark as the midnight sky and loved to fight.

One day, some guys down the hill were jumping Dirty Red and George. It was five against two and they were getting the best of Dirty and George, that was until Rab jumped in and started body slamming the boys to the ground so hard that they could not get back up. When the odds were even the other three boys took flight leaving their buddies to be stumped out.

From that day forward Dirty, Rab and George were a team. They were inseparable, with Dirty being the unofficial leader. Even though they were the same age, Dirty became a mentor to Rab. He taught Rab how important it was to keep his hygiene up. Before Dirty, Rab did not know about haircuts or lineups. He did not wear deodorant, or brush his teeth, and sometimes he would go over a week without taking a bath.

After Dirty got him up to par on his hygiene, he taught him how to dress, all the way down to wearing Polo drawers and socks. Without having any money, Red taught Rab how to get it how he lived. He taught him how to boost clothes and within six months Rab had a new sense of confidence. He smelled better, dressed better and even looked better. Girls started to become attracted to him, and he felt forever indebted to Red.

When Rab got out to the parking lot, Dirty was sitting inside of the car adjusting the radio station. Rab walked around the car appraising it.

"Damn Dirty! It's tight, where did you get it from?"

"My uncle took me to this spot on the west side. Dude got some nice rides over there. When you and George get ready to get a car, I'm going to take y'all over there. Get in we got twenty minutes to get up to South before it lets out."

Rab jumped into the passenger's seat and Dirty pulled out of the lot. He headed up to South High school, where he and Rab were technically still students like George.

They got up to the school and Dirty pulled into the parking lot on the side of the building. That was where most of Garden Valley students would exit the building. Dirty parked and him and Rab got out of the car and sat on its hood. Two minutes later the students started to file out of the school. They immediately noticed Dirty and Rab sitting on the hood of the sparkling Park Ave.

The boys looked at Dirty and Rab with envy, while the girls looked on in awe.

George finally exited the building, with his arm draped around a high yellow girl named Angie. "George!" Dirty yelled out. George looked up and seen Dirty and Rab sitting on the car. He took his arm from around the girl and walked away from her without saying a single word to her.

"My boys!" George said as he approached them.

Dirty and Rab got off of the car and each gave George some dap.

"Who car is this?" George asked as he looked the car over.

"It's mine!" Dirty told him. A group of girls stood close by watching them.

"Ain't that Dirty Red?" Robin asked her friends.

"Yeah, that is his fine black ass." replied fat Monique. They watched Dirty, Rab and George get into the car, with Dirty getting into the driver's seat.

"Dirty done got him a fly car!" Clarissa stated.

"Girl, you better stop being shy and holla at him before some other chick does." Lynn told Robin.

"I ain't approaching no boy and end up getting embarrassed!"

"I will holla at him for you." fat Monique told her.

"A Dirty!" Monique yelled as Dirty drove by leaving out of the lot. Dirty stopped the car put it in reverse and backed up to Monique, who had started walking in the car's direction.

"What's up Monique?" Dirty asked her when she was next to his window.

"My girl Robin likes you. She has been digging you for a minute, but is too shy to approach you."

"Oh yeah, what's her number? I'm going to get at her thick dark ass." Monique pulled a pen and a piece of paper out of her purse, wrote Robin's number down, then passed it to Dirty.

"Tell her I said to be expecting a call from me." he told Monique as he put the car back into drive and pulled off.

Monique walked back over to her friends, "What did he say?" asked Robin.

"I gave him your number and he told me to tell you that he is going to get at your thick dark ass." Robin broke into a wide grin, "He said it like that?"

"He said it just like that. Now come on smiley face before we miss our bus." Monique told her. They all headed for their school bus.

Ÿ

Dirty drove down to the King Kennedy projects and turned onto Bundy drive, which was known as the wet strip. He pulled over in front of apartment building BI5. Old school Tex was sitting outside on a lawn chair, listening to a portable radio. Dirty blew his car horn, and Tex got up and strolled towards his car. When he got to it, he leaned inside of the passenger's side window.

"Tex, you got some of that good shit?" Dirty asked him.

"I got that star trek that beam you up."

"Let me get two joints."

"I will be right back." Tex headed into his house, went into his freezer and pulled out a small package that was wrapped inside of aluminum foil. Tex opened the foil and took out two wet joints. He refolded the foil, placed it back into the freezer then headed back outside. He got to the car and passed the joints to dirty, who in return passed him a twenty dollar bill. Dirty then pulled off and drove down to Outhwaite Estates, another project down the way. He pulled up in front of P.O.C's recreation center, where everyone would hang out after school. He parked in front of the basketball court. Everyone was looking at the car as it parked, wondering who was inside of it.

Dirty nor his crew got out of the ear, instead Dirty rolled up his power windows and turned on the car's air conditioning. He pushed in the car's lighter and when it popped out he lit up one of the wet joints. He took three deep pulls, and then passed the joint to Rab, who also took three deep pulls before passing it to George. George did not really like smoking wet. Just to fit in, he would take light puffs and never fully inhale the smoke. He figured that someone out of the three of them needed to keep their senses, when the others got high.

The guys at the court started to get suspicious, after the car sat there running for over ten minutes without anyone getting out of the car.

Mike told Ron. "Let's go and see who them niggas is." Ron pulled a small twenty two out of his pocket and said, "Come on." They walked over to the car and Mike tapped on the driver's side window, while Ron stood back clutching the gun. Dirty rolled his window down and the strong smell of PCP and smoke escaped out of the window. Once the smoke cleared, they had seen that it was Dirty Red.

"Red what's up?" Mike said. Red just sat there smiling, he was high and stuck.

"Aye it's Red!" Mike hollered over to the courts.

Bruce, China Man and Keith were all playing basketball. They stopped and walked around the fence. They walked up to Dirty's car.

"This your car?" Bruce asked him. Dirty had his head lying back on his headrest.

"Damn! He had been smoking that skinny Minnie!" Keith said.

"Y'all got some more of that?" Bruce asked. George passed half of the last joint out of the window to him, and then climbed out of the backseat.

"This Dirty's car?" Bruce asked George.

"Yeah, he just got it today."

"Y'all niggas be hitting some sweet licks, we need to be getting with y'all." Bruce stated as he hit the wet joint.

"Come on Dirty!" George said to him as he helped him out of the front seat and placed him into the back. That's why George did not like smoking wet. You could not think or react quickly. He figured that somebody had to be able to watch their backs. Rab was in the front passenger's seat stuck too.

George jumped into the driver's seat and pulled off. Bruce and his crew and Mike and his crew stood there watching, as George pulled off driving Dirty's car.

"Them niggas are getting real money." stated China Man.

"Yeah, they are getting it." said Bruce.

"We need to get down with them." Mike stated as they headed back to the court to finish the game.

Chapter 3

A week later, Dirty went back to his uncle Loft's house. Loft gave Dirty the four thousand that he owed him. Dirty went and paid Rick three more thousand. Rick accepted the money as payment in full. He knocked off the other couple hundred that Dirty owed, for him paying the car off so quickly.

Dirty gave Rab and George five hundred apiece and had only a couple hundred left to his name. He knew that he would need to hit another lick soon. He decided that he would chill for a couple of days, while he figured something out.

He decided to call Robin. He pulled up to a payphone and dialed her number. She was surprised when he called. She had given up on hearing from him after a week had gone by. She figured that he must have already had a girl. It was ten days after Monique had given him her number when he finally called. The phone rang and she answered it, "Hello?"

"Is Robin there?"

"This is she"

"This is Dirty Red. Monique gave me your number and told me that you were trying to get at me."

"Well, it's obvious that you weren't trying to get at me. It took you ten days to call me."

"It wasn't like that, I just been busy trying to handle a few things. I'm all caught up now, so I decided to give you a call. So what's up? I hear that you have been digging me for a while now."

"I do not know what digging you means, but I do think that you are kind of cute."

"Just kind of huh?" Robin giggled then asked, "Do you have a girl-friend?"

"No, I'm solo right now."

"Are you a player?"

"Life is too serious to play anything. I lost my mother a couple years ago. She was only thirty three and that showed me that there ain't no time to be playing games. You have to make every minute count."

"I am sorry to hear about your mother. My mother is not physically dead, but she is mentally and spiritually dead. She is out there walking the streets like a zombie, getting high and selling herself. I live with my grandmother." Dirty felt a connection to her instantly.

He told her, "I live with my grandmother too. Look let's get off of the sad stuff, they got all night skating at USA Saturday are you interested in going with me?"

"Yeah, I would like to go."

"I will pick you up earlier in the day, so that we can catch a movie and get   something to eat before we head to the rink, is that a bet?"

"Yeah, that's cool and tell your boy George that my girl Lynn likes him."

"I will tell him. See if she wants to go to the rink too. We can do a little double date."

"Okay, I will ask her but I am sure that she is going to want to go."

"I got a couple moves to make. I might come up to the school and pick you up one day this week."

"What day?"

"I can't tell you, it will be a surprise."

"Yeah whatever, bye!" Robin told him then hung up. Dirty hung up the phone and sat there daydreaming about Robin. She was just dark as him, but she had flawless skin. She was very pretty and had pearly white teeth. She also had a body that was beyond her years.

Dirty wondered if she was still a virgin. He knew that it was a slim chance. Girls from the projects usually lost their virginity by the time that they turned thirteen. Robin was in the eleventh grade, so she had to be at least sixteen or seventeen. He had never heard anybody from the hood brag about hitting her, so he thought that maybe he could make her the one for him.

He decided to shift his focus, because he needed some money. He pulled away from the payphone and drove around trying to figure out what his next lick would be.

Ÿ

Bruce, China Man and Keith were in the Longwood plaza. They had just gotten an old head to cop them a forty ounce of Old English beer. They were about to head back across the street to the Green Court projects, when Bruce noticed a Rent-A-Center truck pull into the plaza's parking lot.

"Hold up y'all!" Bruce told his boys. They both stopped and Bruce watched the van park in between two cars. A man got out of the van and headed into the SavMor grocery store.

"I bet that van got some shit in it, come on." he said to his boys as he took off in the direction of the van. Bruce walked in between the van and the car parked next to it, and peered inside of the window. He has seen that there was stereo equipment, TV's and a washer and dryer.

"Bingo!" He said as he pulled his screwdriver out and busted the door lock. He then opened the back door and climbed inside. Once inside, he opened the latch on the other back door and flung it open, "Come on y'all!" he yelled to Keith and China man. He looked around the van and seen that it was so much stuff that he did not know where to start. He grabbed a thirteen inch color TV and handed it to China Man, who took off running with it dragging its cord. He gave Keith a four foot tall speaker, by then other people in the plaza had started to take notice as to what was going on and started rushing over there. China Man had carried the TV across the street and gave it to somebody to hold and ran back over to the plaza.

"Y'all get out of the way!" Bruce said to the people that crowded the truck.

"Let me finish and y'all can have what's left!" Bruce rolled a stereo set that sat in a wooden case with a glass door to the back door of the truck. He told China Man to grab the bottom of the case and they lifted it out onto the ground. Bruce jumped out of the truck and the crowd of people that were standing there jumped in. Bruce and China Man were rolling the stereo system, when they heard someone yell, "Hey, y'all get out of there!"

Bruce looked back and seen the man in the Rent-A-Center uniform rushing towards the van. People were running in every direction with appliances in their hands. "Pick it up!" Bruce told China Man. China Man grabbed the bottom and lifted it up off of the ground. They had the system lying sideways as they tried to run across the street. They dropped the system at least two times while trying to cut through the middle of traffic. The light was green and cars were flying back and forth. Horns blew as cars swerved to keep from hitting them. Once they got to the other side of the street they set the system back down and started rolling it again.

Keith yelled from a hallway window, "Up here!" They pushed the system towards the building that Keith was in. They picked the system up again to carry it up the building's three front steps, and then rolled it into the building.

"Bring it up here to Ms. Matty's house!" Keith yelled down to them.

"Shit! You are going to have to come and help us, this motherfucker is heavy!" Bruce yelled back up to him. Keith came trotting down the stairs, "Damn! Y'all some weak ass niggas."

"Just get in the middle Arnold dumb ass nigga." China Man said laughing.

They all carried the stereo system up to the third floor of the apartment building. When they got to the top landing they all were sweating and breathing hard even Keith.

"What's wrong Hulk?" China Man said jokingly to Keith.

"Shit ain't so light is it?" Bruce asked him.

"Okay, I was wrong, that shit is heavy!" Keith admitted to them. A door opened, and a silver haired old lady with no teeth in her mouth appeared in the door way, "Y'all hurry up and get that thing in here before someone sees you." Ms. Matty told them as she backed up out of the doorway, so that they could roll the system into her house.

The boys had a thirteen inch Zenith color television and a Panasonic stereo system with one speaker.

"What do you boys want for that stuff?" Ms. Matty asked them. Bruce told her, "Give us five hundred dollars for it all." Ms. Matty let out a wicked cackle, pulled out a Virginia slim cigarette, lit it, took a puff then said, "Y'all might as well take that shit back outside. Ain't no way I'm giving you five hundred dollars for that bullshit!" Bruce became pissed that they had carried all that shit up there to her house, and then she started tripping. He knew that she had the money. Her old innocent looking ass, sold all the pills in the neighborhood, and she made good money from it.

"So, how much are you willing to give us?" Bruce asked her, not wanting to have to carry all that stuff back downstairs and out into the open.

"I will give y'all three hundred."

"Come on Ms. Matty, you know that you are playing us."

"Boy that's some cheap shit, plus you only got one speaker for the stereo. Three hundred or get that hot ass shit up out of here." Bruce looked at Keith and China Man who both hunched their shoulders.

"Yeah, you got that, give us the three hundred." Bruce told her. Ms. Matty reached into her bra, unhooked a safety pin and pulled out a dingy rolled up sock. She unrolled the sock and pulled out a knot of money out of it. She counted out three hundred dollars and handed it to Bruce, who in turn handed Keith and China Man a hundred dollars apiece.

"Nice doing business with you young fellas." Ms. Matty told them as she escorted them to the door. They all filed out of her apartment. Bruce was the last one to exit and mumbled under his breath, "Old hag."

"What was that you said?" asked Ms. Matty.

"I said I lost my bag."

"Yeah, that's what I thought you said!" Ms. Matty said to him then slammed her door.

Bruce, Keith and China Man all broke out laughing as they headed downstairs.

"So, what's up now?" China Man asked.

"We need to find us a ride out to the rink for this Saturday. It's going to be all night skating." Bruce told them.

"If we give Tuffy some gas money and pay his way into the rink, he will take us, I bet." Keith said to them.

"Okay, let's go and see if we can find that nigga." Bruce said

Chapter 4

After not being able to come up with a lick, Dirty decided to go up to the Omens motorcycle club. The Omens were one of three motorcycle clubs that leased buildings and held weekly events that everybody who was somebody would attend. All the high rollers, high cappers and gold diggers would show up at the weekly events.

Sometimes after the clubs would close down, they would all head down to Orange Street next to the freeway. There members from the different clubs would bet on everything from racing to who could ride the longest willy. This would go on usually until the cops showed up to shut it down.

The Omens held their weekly gathering inside of an old abandoned factory that the club had bought. The second floor of the factory was just a big open space. They had a couple of pool tables and video games for the patron's enjoyment. They also had a few couches and chairs scattered throughout the second floor. There was DJ equipment set up in a corner, where a DJ would keep the house rocking.

The parking lot for the Omens was a big field that was across the street from the factory. Lots of people would just hang out in the parking lot and mingle. Cars would have their fog lights on and music playing, while guys sat on their car hoods and tried to knock off the girls that were entering the club.

Dirty pulled up and found a parking spot. He parked, cut his car off and got out of it. He was crossing the street heading to the club, when someone yelled his name out, "Hey Dirty Red!" Dirty stopped and turned in the direction that the voice had come from. He seen that it was Hobo and started walking in his direction.

Hobo was sitting on the hood of a '78 Caprice Classic that was sitting on whale rims and white wall tires.

When Dirty got there Hobo told him, "Dirty, I got somebody that I want you to meet. This right here is Cadillac Lou." Dirty looked at the man that was standing next to Hobo. He was a short fat man that was dressed in Louis Vuitton all the way down to his shoes. He was also draped in diamonds and gold.

"What's up my man? I have been hearing a lot of good things about you." Lou told Dirty while sticking his hand out. Dirty reached out and shook his hand and said, "Yeah, like what?"

"Like that you are a thorough young nigga who likes getting money."

"Money makes the world go around." Dirty responded.

"You got that right, but listen are you trying to make some real money?"

"Always!"

"Let's go sit in my car where we can talk in private." Lou told Dirty.

"Okay." Dirty responded as he followed Lou to a Black and gold Cadillac Fleetwood. Right then he knew why they called him Cadillac Lou.

They climbed into the car and Dirty took in how plush the car was. Lou pulled out a joint and started lighting it up. Dirty thought it was just a regular joint, until the peculiar smell of PCP started to fill the air.

"You smoke water?" Dirty asked him.

"Yeah, I smoke a little bit every now and then, truthfully I sell it."

"You sell joints or bottles?"

"Dirty, I sell gallons of juice. Whatever you choose to do in life always do it big, I hear that you have been getting paper, but some little paper. I want to give you a chance to make some real money."

"And why would you want to see me get some real money and you don't even know me?" Lou passed Dirty the joint then said, "Because me seeing you get money is going to also put money into my pockets. Everything is always done for a reason."

"Okay, so what's up?"

"Jewelry!"

"What about jewelry?" Dirty asked.

"There is a lot of money in jewelry right now, especially in gold and diamonds. There is a big market for chains, dookie ropes, herringbones and rings right now."

"Okay so?"

"So, there are a lot of jewelry stores throughout the city. Some of them are small and have no security. Most have showcases that be full of jewelry. All you need is a couple of guys to go in with you. Y'all will each have hammers that y'all will use to smash in the cases and bags to put the jewelry in."

"It's that simple huh?" asked Dirty.

"It's going to take a little more ironing out and a little bit more planning, but yeah it is going to be simple, when we get it altogether."

"Where does the we come in at?"

"Dirty we are going to be a team. I am going to case the spots, give you the layouts and the best escape routes. Also I am going to fence all of the jewelry that you get. When it comes to getting real money Dirty, certain people have to come together to play certain positions. 1 got the knowhow and the connections to get rid of the jewelry and you have the heart and leadership skills to put together a crew of hungry cats that are willing to get money. Together we can all get paper."

Dirty took another hit of the wet, and then passed it back to Lou, "You got a number?" Dirty asked him.

"Yeah, I'm going to give you my home number and my pager number. I am going to need to hear back from you within a week or I am going to have to shoot my shot somewhere else. Dirty I recognize that you are a young thorough nigga and I would like to get money with you. Always remember this, time is money. The more time that passes the more money that is missed, so get at me." Lou told Dirty as he opened his car door and got out, Dirty followed suit.

Lou went back to join Hobo and Dirty headed into the club. Dirty paid the two dollar entry fee and went inside.

The wet that he had smoked with Lou had started to take effect. It was potent and Dirty started to drift into another world. A solemn mood started to overtake him and he started to feel depressed. He was having thoughts about his mother. The dark setting of the club threw him into a dark mood. He went and stood off in a corner.

Tonya and her girl Tina were in the Omens. Tonya was a couple of years older than Dirty Red. She had gone to school with his older brother Lay Lay. She had always thought that Dirty was cute, but that he was too young. She had recently started to hear that Dirty was out in the streets getting money, and even had bought a nice car, not no raggedy one like most young guys be doing.

"Tina ain't that Dirty Red over there?" Tonya asked her. Tina looked over towards the direction in which she was pointing.

"Yeah, that looks like his slope headed ass."

"Girl, don't be talking about my future husband." Tonya said then started walking in Dirty's direction. Dirty was standing in the corner like a zombie. He stood stiff, with no movement at all. Tonya approached him, "Hey Dirty!" Dirty's eyes were glazed over as if he did not even notice her presence.

Tonya could tell that he was high off of something.

"Are you alright?" she asked him. Dirty finally focused in on her and tears started running from the corner of his eyes.

"Damn, he must be fucked up!" Tonya said to herself as she walked back over to Tina.

"Girl Dirty is high off of something. He is over there crying and shit."

"That nigga is probably on that Sheeba Sheeba."

"What the hell is Sheeba Sheeba?"

"That wet! PCP!"

"Well come help me with him. I want to make sure that he gets home safe."

"Girl! You are tripping. I'm trying to find a guy with the perfect combination, a big dick and a lot of money."

"Bitch! Just help me make sure that he is alright."

"Damn Tonya come on. You act like that nigga is your man or some-thing!" Tina said smirking. She followed Tonya back over into the corner, where Dirty was standing. Tonya reached out and grabbed Dirty's hand. He just looked at her, "Dirty are you alright?" she asked.

"My car, take me to my car."

"Yeah girl, that nigga is wet out!" Tina told Tonya.

Tonya led Dirty out of the club and over to the parking lot.

"Where is your car Dirty?" Dirty let go of Tonya's hand and headed in the direction of his car, with Tonya and Tina following behind him. Amazingly Dirty went right to his car, but he could not determine which one of the keys unlocked the car door. Tonya seen him struggling and went to help him. She seen that he was trying to open the car door with a house key. She knew then that he would not be able to drive the car. She took the keys out of his hand and led him around to the passenger's side. She used the key to unlock the door. She opened the door and helped Dirty inside.

She turned to Tina, "1 got it from here!"

"Girl, are you sure? I can follow y'all."

"No, go ahead and get your groove on, I will call you tomorrow, I got this!"

"Alright girl, you be safe." Tina told her then turned and strutted back over to the club.

Tonya got into the driver's seat, adjusted it, then put the key into the ignition and started the car. She pulled out of the lot then turned to Dirty and asked him, "Where do you live?" Dirty's head was, down with his chin on his chest. Tonya realized that he was too out of it to give her directions, so she decided to take him to her house.

She drove to her house on 93rd and Fuller. She pulled Dirty's car into her driveway and cut the car off.   She got out of the car, went and unlocked her door, and then she went and helped Dirty out of the car. He draped his arm around her shoulder as she led him into the house. She helped him over to her couch and he flopped down on it.

Tonya left him there and went into her bedroom. She grabbed a night gown and went into the bathroom to remove her make up. She removed her makeup and changed into her nightgown, then headed back out to the living room. When she got there she was surprised to see that Dirty was no longer on the couch. She checked the kitchen and he wasn't there either. The only other place that he could be was her bedroom. She walked into her bedroom and there was Dirty sprawled across her bed. He had stripped down to his boxers and socks. Tonya just smiled, clicked off the lights and climbed under the cover and went to sleep.

Ÿ

About six in the morning Dirty woke up having to take a piss. He opened his eyes, raised up onto his elbows and looked around the room. He had no idea as to where he was at. He sat up and tried to get his senses in order. His high had gone down, but he was still feeling off balance. He stood up and almost fell. He sat back down for a minute.

Once he got his bearings he stood back up and walked out of the bedroom in search of the bathroom. He found it, went inside, lifted up the toilet seat and took a long strong piss. He pissed for nearly two minutes.

When he was through, he still had an early morning hard on. He walked back into the bedroom and looked at the figure that was lying on the bed on her stomach. Her head was turned sideways, lying on a pillow. He walked over to the side of the bed that she was sleeping on and looked at her face. He recognized that it was Tonya. He wondered how he ended up at her house and in her bed. He tried to remember if anything had happened between them, being that he was only in his drawers. He pulled the cover down off of her and seen her naked ass.

Her gown was twisted up around her waist. Her legs were spread open and her pussy was poking out. Dirty took in how beautiful and round her ass was. Her ass was shaped like a beach ball and her pussy looked so inviting to him. Dirty looked down at his self and seen that his dick was rock hard and sticking out the front of his boxers.

He decided to take the boxers off, and then he climbed onto the bed and positioned himself between her legs. He grabbed his dick and guided it to her pussy. He tried to insert the head of his dick inside of her, stretching her open. It was a tight fit and he had to push hard to get the head in. The pressure from her pussy being stretched opened woke Tonya up. She woke up feeling like she was being split open by the bottom end of a baseball bat. Dirty pushed further in and Tonya gasped, "Damn Dirty! What are you putting in me?"

"This is all me baby girl." Tonya could not believe it.

"Ain't no way that a seventeen year old boy got no dick that big!" Tonya thought to herself. She took her hand and reached behind her. Dirty had half of his dick inside of her, but there was still enough left outside of her for her to wrap her hand around it.

"Damn! This young nigga is holding!" she said to herself. She removed her hand from Dirty's dick and he pushed his self all the way into her. Tonya felt full as if she had just finished eating a three course meal.

Dirty started fucking Tonya, hitting her in different motions, in and out side to side and circular motions. Tonya was amazed that he not only had a big dick but also knew how to work it. She came three times, while Dirty was fucking her. When he turned her onto her side and pushed her knees up to her chest, he pounded her hard. She grunted, yelled and moaned in pleasure.

Dirty came inside of her, filling her up like a gas tank. He pumped so much cum into her that it started to leak back out. Dirty pulled out of her and flopped down onto his back.

"Tonya stretched her legs out and rolled onto her back also. She had so many thoughts racing through her head.

Dirty snapped her back, "Do you got a washcloth so that I can clean myself up?" he asked her.

"Oh yeah, I will get you one." Tonya told him, then got up out of the bed and headed into the bathroom. She grabbed a washcloth off of the towel rack, went to the sink, turned on the hot water, grabbed the soap and started to lightly soap the rag up. She then headed back into the room, sat on the bed next to Dirty, grabbed his dick with one hand and used the other hand to wash him up. After cleaning his dick she lifted his balls up and cleaned them also. She held his balls in her hand longer than necessary, liking the weight of them.

Dirty just laid there nonchalantly. Once Tonya finished cleaning him she asked him, "Are you hungry?" Dirty realized that he was actually starving, "Yeah, I could go for something to eat."

"Okay, let me go and get cleaned up, then I will fix you something to eat." She told him.

Tonya went into the bathroom and took a quick shower, and then she went into the kitchen and cooked some bacon, eggs and pancakes. She took Dirty his breakfast in bed. She sat on the bed and ate her food also. As she sat there and ate, she thought about what was going to be up with her and Dirty. She wanted to know what they did mean.

"So Dirty what's up?"

"What do you mean what's up?"

"I mean between us, I don't be just fucking anybody." Dirty thought about how tight her pussy was.

"Yeah I can believe that. What do you want it to be with us?"

"Well shit! I want you to be my man. You can even stay with me if you want, I will give you a key."

"This is all kind of fast Tonya. Let's just take it slow and see what happens, deal?" Those were not the words that Tonya wanted to hear, but she told him, "Deal!"

Dirty finished eating, got dressed and left promising Tonya that he would return.

Chapter 5

It was Saturday and everyone was getting ready for the all night skating event that was going to be held at USA skating rink out in Wickliffe, Ohio. Dirty picked Robin up about four o'clock, and took her downtown to Tower City to watch a movie. After that he took her to eat at Long John Silvers. After they had eaten, Dirty headed to pick up George. While they were there, Robin called Lynn to tell her that they were on their way to pick her up.

Dirty drove over to Lynn's parking lot and Robin went to go and get her. She and Lynn cattle walked back to the car.

"That's a bad bitch!" Dirty said to George who sat in the back seat cheesing.

Lynn was mixed with something, but nobody knew what it was that she was mixed with. Her hair was long, black and curly, like she had some Spanish in her. Her eyes were slanted, giving her an Asian appearance. Whatever it was that she was mixed with, everybody agreed that she was beautiful. With her banging body, she was a complete ten.

"Robin opened the door and lifted up the front seat so that Lynn could climb into the back with George. Once she was in Robin got into the front seat and Dirty pulled out of the parking lot. He put in an Eric B and Rakim cassette tape into his Alpine stereo system. George started talking to Lynn, "You feeling my style huh?"

"Dag, you ain't conceded is you?" she asked him.

"I'm not conceded I'm just confident."

"You must think that you are some type of player or something?"

"No, I don't think that I'm a player, I control the game." George said to her smiling. She noticed how white his teeth were. She liked George, but she knew that he was trouble. She told herself that after that night they would never kick it again.

Dirty jumped onto the freeway and headed east on 90. He drove out to 305 and Wickliffe, and then got off of the freeway. He drove two blocks then turned into the parking lot of a plaza. He drove to the back of the plaza where the skating rink was located. It was massive commotion. The parking lot of the rink was filled to capacity. The Wickliffe police were up there directing traffic and making sure that no violence broke out.

Dirty could not find a parking spot in the rink's parking lot, so he had to park somewhere else in the plaza. They all got out of the car and walked back down to the rink, and got in line. The line wrapped all the way around to the back of the building. It took them forty five minutes to get in. Once inside they found out that there was barely any elbow room.

Inside of the rink the lights were dim and the music was blaring. There was a live DJ spinning the records. In the middle of the rink was the dance floor. People that wanted to dance had to either wait for the music to stop or take the chance of getting hit by a skater trying to get to the dance floor.

Dirty and his crew found a spot over by the video games and posted up.

Bruce, Keith and China Man were in the middle of the dance floor. They were amped up yelling out there hood down the way. A hood that most people feared. They were not on the dance floor dancing. They were out there making their presence felt. They were pushing and elbowing their way through the dancers, daring anyone to say something. They knew that they were not the only people from down the way in the rink.

Down the way consisted of five different projects that all ran down one street. You had the 30th Estates, Longwood, Outhwaite Estates, Green Court and King Kennedy. During idle times those projects would beef amongst each other. Anything outside of their radius and they would unite.

They had a whistle that was universal through all five projects. If anyone felt beef and gave that whistle, down the way cats would come out of the woodwork.

Bruce and his crew knew that there were a lot of down the way niggas in the rink, so they acted reckless, yearning for something to pop off.

Chapter 6

Tim, Ron and Mike were out in the parking lot terrorizing the cars. They had stolen a car and driven out there. So far they had broken into at least ten cars and removed their stereo systems. They would take turns watching out for the police and the rink's security that was patrolling, while the other two would creep in between the cars peeping into them to see what kind of stereo systems the cars had.

Besides the radios they had found other things also. They came across a .32 automatic firearm a couple of coats and a bunch of cassette tapes. It was only 1am and the rink did not close until six o'clock, so they still had plenty of time to break into as many cars as they could.

There was a click of E.C. teenagers at the rink. East Cleveland was a suburb that had deteriorated into a ghetto. The guys from out there felt that they had something to prove. Just like the down the way teenagers, they started trouble everywhere that they went.

About ten of them stepped onto the rink's floor, heading to the dance floor. They were pushing and tripping the skaters as they went by. They made it to the dance floor and started pushing their way through the dancers, screaming E.C.

Bruce seen them making their way through the crowd, Bruce got up close to China Man's ear, "Them bitch ass E.C. niggas are up in here. Go and tell the hood to come out here on the dance floor. Tell them it's on!" China Man took off across the rink's floor dodging in between the skaters. He went up to the front of the rink where the arcade games were. That is where all the down the way niggas were posted up at. He approached the down the way cats. He told them that it was a bunch of E.C. niggas out on the dance floor tripping. The word started spreading like a wildfire and before you knew it there was a pack of fifty teenagers storming across the rink's floor. When Bruce seen them approaching he started yelling, "E.C. niggas are pussies!"

The E.C crew headed in his direction. The down the way crew had been picking up anything that they could get their hands on, on their way to the dance floor. Some had skates, some had bottles and some even had miniature bowling balls.

The down the way crew pushed through the dance floor parting it like the Red sea. Everyone in the rink could sense that something was going down. People started standing on benches looking towards the dance floor. The DJ even stopped the music and started talking into the microphone, "Please y'all do not start any trouble. If you do they are going to close the place down, just chill!"

By the time the E.C. crew had made it to Bruce, they found them-selves surrounded.

"What's up with you bitches?" Bruce said to them.

"Nigga this E.C., you the bitch!" said a boy about the age of nineteen, who was at the forefront of the E.C. crew.

"This down the way bitch ain't no way to do it, but how down the way do it!" Bruce told him.

"What's up then?" asked the boy that was leading the E.C. crew.

"This is up nigga!" Bruce said and swung on him and all hell broke out. It was fifteen E.C. niggas going against fifty of the grimiest niggas in the city. The down the way crew was beating them to a pulp. They were stomping them and beating them in the head with skates, and dragging them around the rink's floor.

Security and the police rushed into the rink trying to restore order. Because of the panic inside of the rink, the fire and emergency doors had to be opened to keep people from being trampled while trying to exit the building.

Dirty, Robin, George and Lynn flowed with the crowd out through the fire exit. Once outside they seen that several fights had broken out and people were running in every direction. Dirty and the rest of his group calmly walked through the parking lot, carefully avoiding any of the disputes that were taking place.

Bruce, Keith and China Man were in the middle of stomping someone out, when Bruce noticed Dirty and his crew walk by, "A Dirty!" he yelled out. Dirty stopped and looked in his direction. Bruce left Keith and China Man to finish stomping out the helpless individual that was lying on the ground and jogged over to Dirty.

"Dirty what's up man?" he said hyped up.

"About to head back down the way that's all, what's up with you though?"

"Shit, me and my dudes are trying to get down with you and start getting some real money. We are tired of hitting petty ass licks. We are down to put in work." Dirty noticed that Bruce's lip was busted. He could tell that he had been fighting.

"Bruce, me and my niggas are into getting money, we ain't into all that wilding out, fighting and shit. We can get money, but anything that don't add up to getting money, we ain't on. That extra shit, y'all are going to have to leave it alone."

"Say no more, when can we get up with you?"

"Y'all be at P.O.C. everyday right?"

"Yeah, that is our hang out spot."

"Okay, so Thursday or Friday I am going to come up there and holla at y'all about a lick and we will go from there."

"That's a bet, see you then." Bruce said to Dirty then headed back over to where Keith and China Man were in the midst of stomping someone else out.

"Let that nigga go, and let's roll!" Bruce told them. Keith gave the guy one last kick to his ribs before he walked off. They went to Tuffy's car and tapped on the window to wake him up so that he could unlock the door. Tuffy had stayed in the car the whole time that they were in the rink. He had agreed to take them out to the rink if they gave him gas money and put a couple of dollars in his pockets. He did not want to go into the rink and had decided to stay out in the car instead.

Tuffy woke up from the knocking on the window. He seen that it was Bruce and his boys and started unlocking the doors. They climbed into Tuffy's Grand Torino and headed back down the way.

Chapter 7

Dirty was on the freeway heading down the way, when George asked him, "So you really are going to fuck with them cats?"

"Maybe, I met someone who wants to put us on to some bigger licks, and we are going to need more people to pull them off. Bruce might be wild, but he got a lot of heart. Him and his boys are not afraid to get money, so I might see what they are about." Dirty said as he drove.

Ÿ

Mike, Ron and Tim were also on the freeway heading back down the way. They had taken seventeen radios, five equalizers, eight jackets and a whole bunch of cassette tapes. They left a lot of people at the rink mad as hell. Some had their door locks busted while others had their car windows busted, with glass lying all over their front seats. Most of the people could not understand how their car had gotten broken in, with there being security patrolling the lot. A few of the people filed reports, while others just accepted the loss and headed home.

Mike, Ron and Tim already had someone in mind that would by all of the radios, they just hoped that they made it safely back down the way, without the police getting behind them. They were riding in a stolen car full of stolen merchandise, plus the back seat window of the car was broken out. Ron was driving, and he was very nervous. He drove the car as steady as he could.

Dirty exited the freeway on 30th and Woodland. He rode up Woodland until he got to 55th, then turned onto Kinsman and headed up to Garden Valley. He dropped Lynn off first, who seemed very anxious to get away from George.

She and George hadn't said over two words on the ride back home. Dirty knew that George had over played his hand. Lynn wasn't the type of girl that you could high cap on to get her. George was going to have to bring it down a notch. Dirty figured that when they were alone he would put him up on game.

After Lynn, he dropped George off, telling him that he would get with him later on that day. He then drove to Robin's house and parked in front of it.

"Did you have a nice day?" Dirty asked her.

"Yeah, it was great except for the fight that broke out at the rink."

"Yeah I feel you. I learned that sometimes things are just beyond our control." When Dirty said that, his expression turned somber. Robin thought that he was referring to and thinking about his mother's passing.

"So, when am I going to see you again?" Robin asked him.

"When do you want to see me again?"

"Can you come and pick me up from school tomorrow?"

"Yeah, I can do that."

"Do you want to kiss me before I go?" Dirty felt awkward he wasn't really the affectionate or romantic type, but he thought fuck it, and leaned over and gave her a kiss on her lips. It was just a small peck without any tongue action. Robin was happy with that. She felt good as she got out of the car and walked up onto her porch. Dirty waited until she was safely inside of the house before he pulled off.

☐

Dirty drove down to King Kennedy projects, bought him a wet stick then headed to Tonya's house. She opened her door wearing a sheer nightgown, without any panties and bra on. She did not even wait for Dirty to enter all the way before she turned and headed back into the bedroom. Dirty closed and locked the door, then followed her into the bedroom. Tonya sat on the bed and watched TV. Dirty sat on the other side of the bed and began taking his clothes off. He stripped down to his boxers, and then turned to Tonya, "Let me get a light."

"I don't have no lighter or matches. You got to light whatever it is on the stove. Give it here, and I will go and light it." Tonya took the joint from Dirty and walked to the kitchen. She went to the stove and turned on a pilot. She put the joint into her mouth, she bent down to light it. She puffed it to get it lit. On her first pull a funny taste entered her mouth. She instantly started to feel a numbing sensation in her throat.

She had been smoking weed for almost ten years and had never smoked anything that tasted like that or gave her that type of sensation. She hurried back into the bedroom, taking another long pull on the joint.

"Dirty what type of weed is this?" she asked him giggling.

"Girl this that wet, that skinny Minnie!"

"Skinny Minnie?" she asked covering her month with one hand. Dirty knew then that she had done more than just light the joint. From the way that she was tripping, it was too late to warn her. He put his feet up on the bed, laid back and smoked.

"Damn I'm getting hot!" Tonya said and then pulled her gown over her head. She stood there naked. Dirty hit the joint and just looked at her. She climbed onto the bed and positioned herself so that her head was at Dirty's waist. She pulled his dick out of his boxers and started to play with it. She acted like she was examining it. All of a sudden she blurted out, "Fuck it!" then lowered her head taking Dirty's dick into her mouth.

Dirty had never gotten his dick sucked before. In the 80's it was hard to find, young black girls that were not prostitutes, who willingly sucked dick. Dirty looked on in amazement as Tonya sucked his dick. The warm sensation that her mouth was giving him, along with the high that he was getting from the wet had him on cloud nine.

Tonya sucked his dick and licked his balls until his legs started to shake. Dirty skeeted into Tonya's mouth. She sucked him dry, burped, and then fell asleep with her face on his dick. Dirty had smoked the joint down to a roach and after it had burned out he sat it on the nightstand and laid there high until sleep set in on him.

Chapter 8

One in the afternoon Dirty awoke to Tonya sitting on top of him, riding him. She was grinding her pussy on his pelvis. Dirty became fully awake. He reached up and pulled Tonya down to him and started sucking her titties. Actually he made love to her titties. He caressed and sucked each one of them, sending shockwaves of pleasure through Tonya's body. She could not believe that a seventeen year old boy was making her feel like that. Dirty rubbed his hands up and down her bare back.

"Damn Dirty!" she whispered into his ear. Dirty rolled her over onto her back. He spread her legs out as far as they could go, and began to pound Tonya's pussy. She panted, moaned and talked to Dirty, "Beat it up baby, show me that you are a grown man." Dirty's answer to her urgings was to pick up his pace and to use more powerful strokes. Tonya took her legs and spread them out, wrapping her hands around her ankles. She started rolling her hips. Dirty had never experienced a girl do that before. He realized that he was not fucking a girl, but that he was fucking a woman, a woman that fucked back.

"I'm almost there. Come on you young big dick mother fucker, put that dick on me!" Dirty found his self sweating as he pounded Tonya. Her words had brought him to the point of no return. He slammed into her one last time and shot his nut up into her. Tonya felt him cumming and wrapped her legs around his back. She put a clamp on him as if she did not want to let him go. She did not know if she was in love or lust with Dirty, but she did know that she cared for him and would do anything that he asked of her.

After Dirty caught his breath, he looked over to the clock on the dresser and seen that it was after one o'clock. He told Tonya, "I got to make a move right quick, let me up." Tonya reluctantly unwrapped her legs from around him.

Dirty went into Tonya's bathroom and took a quick shower. He walked back into her bedroom naked and Tonya just stared at him, still not believing that he wasn't grown yet. Dirty got dressed, pulled a number out of his pocket and picked up her phone. He dialed the number that he read off of the paper. When someone answered he said, "This is Dirty Red and I am calling to speak to Lou."

"Dirty my man, this is Lou, what's up?"

"I was trying to get up with you to discuss what we talked about."

"That's a good look. Meet me up at Hobo's store in one hour and we can go from there."

"Okay, that's a bet!" Dirty told him and then hung up. Dirty told Tonya that he would be back.

Ÿ

Dirty left to pick up George and Rab. He picked them up then headed up to Hobo's store. When he got up there Dirty parked, got out of his car and entered the store. Hobo was behind the counter, "Hobo what's up?"

"Hey Dirty, Lou told me that you were meeting him up here, he hasn't gotten here yet. Come on into the back, I want to show you something. Fuzzy, watch the register for me." Hobo told his cousin.

Dirty walked behind the counter and Hobo led him into a back room. It was a storage room with boxes of store products stacked all around it.

Hobo went over to a stack of boxes and began to unstack them until he got to the third to last box. He picked that box up and carried it over to a table and started to open the flaps. He called for Dirty to join him. Dirty walked over to the table and looked into the box. There were packages of cocaine neatly wrapped and stacked inside of the box.

Dirty had no idea as to why Hobo was showing him his stash of drugs. It did not take long for Hobo to tell him why, "Dirty coke is about to be the thing that makes people rich. A new way of getting high off of cocaine is quickly spreading across the United States, and it is bringing in plenty of money. I am telling you this because I know that you are a money getter. I just want you to know that whenever you are ready to get money, without having to take big chances, I can put you on, what do you think?"

"I appreciate it Hobo, but that ain't my thing. Maybe down the line, I might change my way of thinking, but right now I like taking shit. It's not even just the money it's the thrill that I get from taking the white people's shit."

"I feel you I had to shoot my pitch, because I know that you are a true hustler."

"No doubt, it's all good."

"Hobo where you at?" a voice yelled from out front. Hobo knew that it was Lou and yelled back, "I'm in the back." Lou went into the back and was surprised to see that Dirty was already there.

"That's what I like a man that is on time. That tells me a lot about your character. It shows me that you are about business. So are you ready to get this money Dirty?"

"I want to hear your plan, to see if it sounds right."

"Okay, we can do that. The first store that I have in mind is Robinson's jewelry store out in Southgate Mall. By it being out in the suburbs they don't have to buzz you in and out. The crackers feel safe out there. Also the freeway is only two blocks away. Now here is the key it's going to take at least four people to do this job you are going to need a driver, a look out and two people to enter the store and handle business. There are two display cases I am interested in. One has bricks of gold and diamond rings in it and the other has chains in it. Links, herringbones and dookie ropes."

"How are we supposed to get into the cases?"

"Let me finish and I will explain. You and whoever else that goes in with you will have hammers. Also you will have drawstring bags. When the time is right, you will both hit the glass cases, smashing them with the hammers, grab the merchandise, put it in the bags and bounce. You jump into the car and head to the freeway. 480 will lead you down the way. We will meet up and tally up the prices on the jewelry. I will pay you a third of what the total price is, how does that sound?"

"How many people work in that store?"

"It is family owned, a husband and wife team, they are in their late fifties. It will be as easy as slicing a piece of pie with a Ginsu knife."

"And you are going to have the money when we bring you the goods?"

"It wouldn't be right if we did it any other way."

"What's the best day to hit it?"

"Saturday, because it won't be a business day, so there will be less traffic, which makes for an easier getaway. Saturday at around ten in the morning, do we have a deal?"

"I got to get a couple more people on my team. I'm going to call you sometime before Thursday to let you know if everything is a go, is that cool?"

"I will be waiting on your call Dirty." They shook hands and Dirty left the store.

Chapter 9

He got back into his car, started it up and pulled off. He was going over everything in his head. He was envisioning the whole heist. He decided that he needed to see the store and the getaway route. He headed out to Maple Hts., where Southgate Mall was located.

"Dirty, what's up dawg? You been quiet ever since you got back into the car." George said to him.

"I got to figure something out!" was all that Dirty said as he pulled into Southgate's parking lot. He drove around until he found Robinson's jewelry store. He parked the car and sat there watching the store for about fifteen minutes. Then he started to observe the rest of the plaza. He threw the car in drive and pulled out to the other side of the plaza. He turned left and seen the big green freeway sign. He headed to the freeway and got on it. He looked at his Guess watch, when he got on the freeway. He did the speed limit until he got to the 30th and Woodland exit, then he looked at his watch again. Seventeen minutes was all that it took, to get from Southgate to down the way.

He got off the freeway and drove down to Outhwaite Estates. He pulled up in front of the P.O.C. recreation center and seen that it was a basketball game going on. He scoured the court looking for Bruce, but did not see him. Tim and Ron were at the court and decided to approach Dirty.

"Dirty, what's up?" Tim asked him.

"I'm looking for Bruce."

"That nigga up in the plaza, getting some beer." Ron took a pellet out of his pocket and threw it at a bottle that was lying on the ground. The bottle exploded into many pieces. Dirty had witnessed the whole thing.

"Ay! What did you hit that bottle with?" Dirty asked Ron.

"Oh this!" Ron asked Dirty as he pulled another bearing out of his pocket.

"What is that? Dirty asked him.

"This is a wheel bearing. This is what we do our bust & snatches with."

"Could I look at it?" Ron handed the bearing to Dirty who examined it.

"This little pellet can bust a forty ounce bottle?"

"That pellet can bust almost any type of glass. It can bust a car window, a store window it can even shatter windows that have wire running through them." Dirty's mind started turning. He handed the bearing back to Ron, but he knew that one day he would need one of those bearings.

"Alright, let me go up here and holla at Bruce!" Dirty told them then pulled off. Dirty drove around the corner to the plaza and pulled over to the beverage store. There was a small crowd in front of the store shooting dice.

Always at the center of attention, was Bruce in the middle of the crowd. He had a forty ounce of Old English in one hand and a pair of dice in the other.

Dirty threw the car in park and got out of the car. As he was approaching the game he heard someone say, "Shoot the fucking dice nigga!" Bruce responded, "Keep talking nigga and you're going to be the one that I shoot."

"Nigga, you ain't got no gun."

"Nope, I'm going to shoot this straight right to your mouth!" Bruce said, and then rolled the dice. Bruce hit his point then said, "Point seen, money gone!" as he scooped up his winnings.

"You want to bet back nigga?" Bruce asked the man who had lost over two hundred dollars to him.

"Nigga, I ain't fading your shit talking ass no more." Bruce looked round the crowd, "Anymore faders?" he asked.

"Bruce let me holla at you right quick." Bruce looked over and seen Dirty standing there.

"You niggas are lucky." Bruce said as he pushed through the crowd.

"Dirty what's up dawg?"

"I need to holla at you. Get in my car and roll with me." Bruce turned the forty ounce bottle up and downed what was left, leaving only suds in the bottle. He flung the bottle, "Let's roll my nigga." Together they walked back to Dirty's car. Dirty opened his car door and pulled the seat forward, so that Bruce could climb into the back seat. Bruce climbed into the car and said, "What's up George, what's good Rab." They each spoke back. Dirty got into the car and put it in drive and pulled off. Dirty started talking.

"I got a lick set up. it's a jewelry store out in Maple Heights. I already done scoped the spot out and someone has given me all the info that I need to pull it off. There is only room for four people though and if you want it, I am offering you the fourth spot."

"What about my boys? I can't leave them hanging."

"You can throw them something out of your cut and maybe it will be room for them the next time. It's not my call on this, so are you in or out?" Bruce thought for a minute. He knew that Dirty was giving him the opportunity of a lifetime, and there wasn't any way that he was turning it down. He figured that his boys would just have to understand.

"I'm in for sure."

"Okay, it's going down Saturday morning, so I am going to need to pick you up at about eight o'clock in the morning."

"Just pick me up in front of P.O.C. I will be there waiting. Matter of fact you can drop me off up there right now." Bruce told Dirty. Dirty drove up to P.O.C and pulled in front of the courts. He opened his door and raised his seat up allowing Bruce to get out, "See you Saturday!" Dirty told him before pulling off.

Tim and Ron seen Bruce get out of Dirty's car and approached him, "Dirty about to put you down?" Ron asked him.

"Yeah, we are about to do a little something."

"We are trying to get down too,"

"Shit, it ain't even no room for my boys to get down right now, but he did say that it might be some bigger licks coming up, if so I will tell him about y'all!"

"That's cool." Tim told him. Bruce walked around the other side of the fence.

"Who got next?" he asked trying to play a game of basketball.

Ÿ

Dirty drove up to the Valley looking for Donny. He was going to need him to get him a car for the lick. He rode through the Valley asking everybody had they seen Donny. Nobody had seen him.

Dirty knew that there wasn't any telling where Donny could be, he was a wild one. Donny did everything under the sun. He stole cars, robbed people, burglarized houses, and he did not care who he victimized. Every other day either someone was shooting at him or it was the other way around.

Donny would hear that someone was looking for him and pop up out of nowhere, surprising the person that was supposed to be looking for him. Dirty figured that the best bet would be to put the word out that he was looking for Donny and let Donny find him.

He started telling everybody that he could to tell Donny that he was looking for him.

It was Sunday and Dirty was low on money. It was six days until they were to hit the lick. He needed gas money and spending money.

"I need y'all to let me hold a hundred dollars apiece." he told George and Rab. He knew that they still had some money because they did not have anything to spend it on. They stole damn near everything. They both pulled knots out of their pockets and peeled off a hundred dollars and handed it to Dirty.

"Y'all want to roll down to the funky spot?" Dirty asked them.

"Yeah, that bitch be jumping on Sundays!" Rab said referring to the Mad Hatter, which was also known as the funky spot. The Mad Hatter was a club in downtown Cleveland. It was an eighteen and older club, but sometimes exceptions were made. The Mad Hatter had a live DJ, sold liquor and had two floors. People from all over the city would attend. Once the Hatter got packed to capacity, the partying would over flow to outside of the club. The parking lot and the one way street that it sat on would be packed with people.

Dirty headed down there. He pulled up to 18th and Prospect and seen that the Hatter was jumping just as they had expected. Cars lined the street and people were standing on both sides of the streets. Dirty turned onto the street and turned off his headlights. He cruised down the street with just his park lights on.

Though Dirty was only seventeen, everybody knew him because he boosted and sold clothes. He always somehow showed up everywhere something was jumping and his trusted two partners were always at his side.

Dirty pulled into the parking lot, threw his car in park and got out. George and Rab followed him. They all posted up on the hood of Dirty's car. People started to pull up and give Dirty dap and props on his car.

There were a lot of down the way cats up there and they all gave Dirty some type of recognition. A couple of people approached him and asked him if he had any clothes for sale. Dirty advised them that he was no longer in the boosting clothes business. He informed them that starting the next week he would be in a new line of business.

They chilled down there until midnight. Dirty had not been home to his grandmother's house in almost a week. He decided that he would stay there that night so that his grandma Pearl would know that he was alright.

He dropped Rab and George off, and then headed over to the west side to his house. When he got there, everyone was asleep. He went into him and Dodee's room. He stripped his clothes off and climbed under the cover on his bed and instantly fell asleep. Dirty had been ripping and running the streets so much that it had taken a toll on him, he slept until noon.

Ÿ

When he awoke he smelled the aroma of food cooking. He knew that his grandma Pearl was in the kitchen cooking.

He went into the bathroom and took a hot bath. He then went back into his room and got dressed. He put on some Levi's 501's, a blue Polo shirt, and a pair of Air Jordans on his feet. He switched his guess watch for a swatch watch, and then headed into the kitchen.

Ms. Pearl was at the stove boiling greens and ham hocks. She turned when Dirty entered the kitchen, "The lord must of had mercy, he answered my prayers. Boy, where have you been? I have been worried sick about you."

"I been down in the Valley with George and Rab. You don't have to worry about me grandma."

"Child, if your mother knew how you done took to them streets, she would turn over in her grave. You need to stay out of the streets Tyrone, before you end up like your daddy."

"I will never be like him granny, never! Could I have something to eat before I go?"

"You are about to leave already? When am I going to see you again, when I'm in my casket?"

"Come on grandma, I will be back tonight."

"You haven't even seen your brothers have you?"

"No, I haven't seen them. I know that Dodee has been staying over to Aunt Lois' house and Lay Lay been staying down at his girl's house in King Kennedy."

"Y'all need to be looking out for each other." Ms. Pearl told him as she fixed him a plate of pork chops, rice and string beans.

Dirty knew that Lay Lay would be alright, but he did worry about Dodee from time to time. He knew that he needed to check up on him soon. Dirty pulled a hundred dollars out of his pocket and gave it to his grandmother, "Boy, where is you getting this type of money from?"

"Don't worry about it just get you and Dodee something. He finished eating his food, dumped the leftovers into the trash and put the plate in the sink. He told Ms. Pearl, "I will see you later." He bent down and gave her a kiss on her cheek, then left.

Chapter 10

He got into his car and headed up to South High to pick up Robin. When he got up to there, school was just letting out. Dirty pulled into the parking lot and got out of   his car. He stood outside of it as the kids filed out of school. Robin and her click finally exited the building, "There go Dirty!" Lynn said to Robin, they all stopped. Robin told them, "I will see y'all later."

"Gone and get you some dick girl!" fat Monique said teasingly to her.

"Girl you are so nasty." Robin replied as she took off walking in Dirty's direction. When she got to Dirty he asked her, "Are you ready?"

"Yeah, I'm ready." Robin told him then walked around to the passenger's side and got in. Dirty got into the car and was about to pull off when George called out to him, "That's how you are going to do your boy?"

"Come on!" Dirty yelled out the window to him. George jogged over to the car and climbed into the back seat.

"I'm dropping you off somewhere." Dirty told him.

"That's cool just drop me off at the rec center." George then asked Robin, "Your girl Lynn ain't feeling me no more huh?"

"She likes you, but she knows that you are a player and she ain't with that."

"One day she will get with the program, they all do." George said then sat back. Dirty dropped George off at the Garden Valley rec center, and then pulled back off.

"You hungry?" he asked Robin.

"A little bit!" she responded. Dirty drove to McDonald's and got each of them a quarter pounder with cheese combo and a chocolate shake. Dirty then headed back over to the west side. He went back home.

When he entered the house Ms. Pearl was sitting at the kitchen table watching a little portable black and white TV that was sitting on the counter. She smiled, when she seen Dirty enter the house. She was glad that he was back. As long as he was there she knew that he was safe.

"Granny this is my friend Robin."

"How are you doing child?"

"I'm fine." Robin replied shyly.

"You don't have to be shy with grandma Pearl you hear me?"

"Yes ma'am."

"Granny we are about to go into my bedroom and watch a movie."

"That's all y'all better be doing in there. I don't want to hear no bed shaking or no bumping on the walls." Ms. Pearl said laughing.

"Yeah whatever, come on Robin." Robin followed Dirty down the hall to his room, which had a set of twin beds, a night stand that held a 19" color TV that had a VCR on top of it. Dirty walked over to the TV and turned it on. He also turned on the VCR, and put the movie Robocop in. He went and sat on the bed, took his shoes off and put his feet up on the bed as he laid down. Robin followed suit, she took off her shoes and laid down on the bed next to Dirty. For some reason she felt at ease with Dirty. She felt comfortable as if she had known him for a long time. She had really just met him, but still felt safe and secure with him.

She didn't know why, but she got the urge to kiss him and she did. Dirty was surprised by her forwardness. Robin's hand went to Dirty's pants. She unbuttoned his Polo belt, and then unbuttoned his pants. She stuck her hand inside of his pants and was shocked at what she felt, "Could that really be all him," she thought to herself.

Dirty took over, he laid Robin down and started French kissing her. His hands found the buttons on her shirt and unbuttoned them. He then undid the buttons of her jeans. Dirty tried to pull her jeans down, but it was hard with her pants being so tight and her lying down.

Robin sat up and took her shirt off. She undid her bra, then stood up and pulled her pants off. She stood there in a pair of flower print panties that had hair sticking out the sides and top of her panties.

Robin was dark as a Hershey's chocolate bar, and she was very hairy. Dirty's dick instantly got hard.

"Pull your panties off!" he told her. Robin stepped out of her panties and stood before Dirty unashamed. Dirty appraised her body, starting at her full, round, ripe titties. They sat up and had big dark nipples. Her stomach was flat and from her navel down she was very hairy.

"Turn around." Dirty told her, and she did. Dirty seen that her ass was shaped perfectly. He stood up and began taking off all of his clothes, and Robin watched him undress.

Unknown to Dirty, this was about to be Robin's first time going all the way. She had been finger fucked before, but never had truly been penetrated. Dirty walked over to her and gently pushed her down onto the bed. Robin laid down and spread her legs. Dirty climbed on top of her and guided his dick to her pussy.

"Go slow this is my first time." she whispered to him.

Dirty did not believe her. He put his dick to her entrance and tried to push it in, but it wouldn't go. Dirty spit into his hand then rubbed the spit around the head of his dick, and then he tried again. It still wouldn't go. He got up off of her and went over to his dresser and grabbed a bottle of Jergen's lotion. He squirted some of the lotion into the palm of his hand, and then rubbed it up and down his dick.

He crawled back onto the bed and put his hand between her legs and lubed her pussy up. He positioned himself between her legs again. This time he got the head in. Robin gasped and closed her eyes. Dirty pushed in further and Robin felt a searing pain shoot through her body. She cried silently, but took it like a big girl. All of a sudden Robin's pussy became real wet, and Dirty was able to slide all the way into her. He fucked Robin, slowly for about two minutes before the pain started to subside. After the pain subsided, pleasure started to replace it and Robin started to respond to it. She started fucking Dirty back, by grinding and rotating her hips.

Dirty lost control and nutted in her faster than he wanted to. It wasn't until he got up off of her that he realized that his whole pelvic area was covered in blood. He looked down at Robin and seen that she had blood in between her thighs. He realized that she had been telling the truth when she told him that she was a virgin.

She was Dirty's first virgin, and that made him feel proud. To him, Tonya was alright, but in Robin he had something pure. He knew that he wasn't going to let her go. She was now officially his.

They each went into the bathroom and cleaned themselves up. Afterwards Dirty replaced the stained sheets that were on his bed, with clean ones. They headed back up front, and Ms. Pearl was sitting in the same spot. She looked up at them and grinned, "It was a good movie huh?" she asked them.

"Very good granny."

"Around this time next year I might be a great grandma." she said giggling.

"Bye Ms. Pearl." Robin said to her as her and Dirty was leaving out of the house.

"Good bye child, you come back and see me you hear?"

"I will." Robin said before Dirty pulled the door closed. Dirty dropped Robin off.

Ÿ

Dirty went to the Valley to check on Rab. No sooner than he pulled into Rab's parking lot and parked his car, his passenger's side door flew open scaring the shit out of him. In jumped Donny smiling, "What's up Dirty? I hear that you have been looking for me." Dirty had to wait for his heart to come back up into his chest, before he said, "Donny man don't be doing that bullshit!"

"I scared you huh? My bad!" Donny said smiling. Dirty thought to his self, "This mother fucker is getting crazier and crazier.

"Look Donny, I need a car for a lick that I got set up for this Saturday."

"Dirty, you haven't straightened me for the last car that I got for you, and now you are riding around in this pretty mother fucker."

"I know your right, I swear I got you."

"We go back to third grade Dirty. I don't want to fall out with you about no money."

"I know how you get down. I swear I got you for both cars after I hit this lick, that's my word."

"What type do you need this time my nigga?"

"It has to be a four door, and it has to be fast in case we get chased. I need to be able to smoke the police if they get behind us."

"When do you need the car?

"We are hitting the lick Saturday morning, so I'm going to need the car by at least Friday night."

"Friday night by midnight there will be a car sitting in this parking space for you. I will see you Monday." Donny told Dirty then jumped out of the car.

"A Donny!" Dirty called out to him. Donny stuck his head back inside of the car's window. "What's good?"

"We ain't seen each other since you got the last car for me, so how did you know that this was my car?"

"Come on Dirty, you might haven't seen me, but I have seen you many times!" Donny told him laughing, then turned and walked away.

"Yeah, that nigga is crazy!" Dirty said to his self.

He got out of the car and went to Rab's house. When Rab let him in, he had seen that George was there also. Dirty told them that Friday night, they were all going to need to stay at Rab's house, so that they would be together the next morning.

Ÿ

For the remainder of the week Dirty split his time up between Tonya and Robin. Tonya had started to become too possessive, wanting to know his whereabouts. She would catch an attitude when Dirty did not stay at her house.

At first Dirty was flattered by her jealousy, then it started to become annoying. Tonya did not realize it, but she was starting to push Dirty away.

One thing that Dirty did not like was to feel like he was being pushed into a corner. That is why he barely stayed at his grandma Pearl's house. Dirty knew that pretty soon he was either going to have to set Tonya straight or cut her off.

Chapter 11

Friday came around and Dirty, Rab and George were all together. They were at the Zulu's motorcycle club. Dirty was just driving through to feel the vibe.

He seen that the *Chevy Boyz* were up there deep that night. The Chevy club consisted of a group of guys that all drove Chevys. They mostly drove Caprices or Impalas which range from 1977 to 1980. They would ride back to back throughout the city.

When they would come to a light the lead car would cut traffic off until all of the Chevys rode through. Donald Ray was the leader of the Chevy club. Dirty's brother Lay Lay used to box with Donald Ray, who was from a rival hood.

Donald Ray flagged Dirty down. Dirty pulled to a stop in front of him.

"Dirty Red what's up?"

"I'm chilling Don."

"You about to go into the club?"

"No, I'm just riding through."

"You need to go ahead and get rid of that Buick and cop you a Chevy, so you can get down with us" Donald Ray told Dirty.

"Shit Don, I'm about to start my own club, called the get money click!" Dirty told him then pulled off smiling.

Ÿ

It was almost midnight, so Dirty headed back to the Valley to see if Donny had come through. He pulled into Rab's parking lot and drove to his usual parking spot. In it sat a four door 1978 Delta 88 Oldsmobile. Dirty pulled into another spot, got out and walked back to the Delta. He walked around the car appraising it. He noticed that there was a folded up piece of paper under one of the windshield wipers. He pulled the paper from under the wiper and unfolded it. He read the paper it read: "I got you, now get me, signed the ghost."

Dirty opened the car door and seen that there was a screwdriver lying on the seat. Dirty picked it up then sat in the driver's seat. He had to find the hole on the side of the steering column. Donny did not do like most car thieves and tear the whole column up. He would make a hole just big enough to stick a screwdriver into it to pull the starting pin up.

Rab and George had gotten out of Dirty's car and were standing outside of the Delta 88 as Dirty stuck the screwdriver into the column and started the car. The car roared to life, it sounded powerful. Dirty checked all of the gauges, and seen that the car had almost a full tank of gas, the transmission and water gauges were normal. He shut the car off, got out and checked all the doors to make sure that they all worked and did not get stuck. Afterward he went over to the trunk of his car, opened it and pulled out a bag. Inside of the bag were four hammers and four drawstring bags that he had purchased from a hardware store earlier in the week. He took the bag and placed it under the front seat of the Delta 88, then he told his boys, "Come on y'all let's go crash." They all headed into Rab's house. They went into his room and found places to crash out.

Dirty woke up about seven o'clock the next morning. He woke up George and Rab, "Come on y'all it's time to go."

They all got up and handled their hygiene then headed out of the house. They got into the Delta and Dirty started it up and pulled off. He drove down the way to 40th and pulled up to P.O.C, and true to his word Bruce was sitting on a bench in front of the center drinking a can of beer. When

Dirty pulled up in front of him, Bruce stood up, downed the rest of the beer then hopped into the back of the car.

"You ready?" Dirty asked him.

"As ready as I will ever be my nigga."

Dirty pulled off, and drove down to 30th and Woodland and jumped onto the freeway.

"Pay attention George, because you are going to be the getaway driver. You need to know this route!" George sat up at full attention, paying close attention to all the signs that they passed on the freeway.

Dirty got off of the freeway on Northfield Road and drove down to Southgate. He entered the mall's parking lot and circled it many times to make sure that it was cool. He looked for the best exit out of the parking lot then he pulled in front of the jewelry store.

"That's it right there. We are going to hit it in about an hour. I'm going to drive over to Gold Circle's parking lot. I don't want to just sit here and start looking suspicious."

Dirty pulled out of the lot and drove over to Gold Circle's department store's parking lot. He pulled into a parking space and started giving them the run down.

"George like I said you are going to be the getaway driver. You are going to back into a parking space and keep the car running. Matter of fact keep the car in drive just keep your foot on the brake. Rab you are going to be the lookout. I want you to stand outside of the store and watch for security patrols. Bruce you are going in with me."

Dirty reached under the seat and pulled out the bag that contained the hammers and the bags. He reached into the bags and pulled out two hammers and two bags. He handed a set to Bruce, "Use that hammer to bust the case and put the shit into that bag. I'm going to tap the counter that I want you to hit when I walk past it, but you don't hit it until I give you the signal. We are going to hit the cases at the same time. You are going to hit for the rings and I am going to hit for the chains. Rab, George, I need some show money. Give me some money to flash so that I can put the white people at ease."

Rab and George both dug into their pockets and pulled out some money and handed it to Dirty. Dirty stuffed the money into his pocket.

He looked at his watch it was 9:45, "It's show time fellas!" Dirty told them as he pulled out of the parking lot and headed back over to Southgate. He pulled into Southgate and backed into a parking spot. He stuck the hammer inside of his waist band and pulled his shirt down over it. He stuffs the bag into his back pocket.

It was ten o'clock and he told them, "Come on y'all." Dirty, Bruce and Rab got out of the car. Rab walked in a different direction than Dirty and Bruce. Dirty pulled the money out of his pocket and held it in his hand as him and Bruce entered the store. There was a middle aged white man standing behind the counter. Dirty wondered where the man's wife was. He quickly scanned the store and spotted the ring case. He walked towards it and as he passed it he tapped it twice, letting Bruce know that it was the one that he wanted him to hit.

Bruce stopped at that case and started looking at the rings as if he intended to purchase one, Dirty kept going.

"Excuse me sir, I am trying to buy a chain." Dirty said to the man as he acted like he was counting the money.

"Well son, do you know what type of chain you are looking for?" The man asked as he greedily stared at the money in Dirty's hands.

"I think I want a size 18" link." The man indicated for Dirty to step down to a display case that was full of chains.

"Look in here and see if there is anything that you like." the man told Dirty.

Dirty looked at the array of chains inside of the display case. He had seen a chain that only cost $199.

"Could I see that chain right there?" Dirty asked the man pointing to the chain. The man slid opens the display case and withdrew the chain.

Dirty looked at the chain. He did not even try it on, before telling the man, "Yeah, I want that, ring it up." The old man smiled then walked over to the cash register to ring the chain up. Dirty pulled the hammer from his waist and winked his eye at Bruce. Simultaneously they hit the display cases shattering them. The old man turned with a shocked expression on his face, and an old white lady came from out of the back yelling, "What's going on!"

"Call the police Helen, we are being robbed!" the old man told his wife.

Dirty knew that they had to hurry. He quickly stuffed as many chains as he could into the bag then ran past Bruce, telling him to come on. Bruce cut his hand deep on a piece of broken glass as he tried to hurry grabbing a brick of rings out of the case.

"Shit!" he said as the pain started to set in. He took off behind Dirty running out of the store. George seen them running out of the store and pulled out of the parking space to meet them. Rab also took off running towards the car they all jumped into the car. The old man had run out of the store and was yelling, "Help!" as George sped off

"Go! Go!" Dirty told George.

George pressed the gas and almost sent the car into a spin as it fishtailed out of the parking lot. Once out of the lot George slowed down and tried to blend in with traffic until he got to the freeway. He jumped onto the freeway and headed down the way. They were all nervous because the man had seen the car. They knew that by now the man had probably given the police a description of the car and that they were looking for it.

"George next time let us come to you, so that they can't get a description of the car or the plate number."

"My fault!" George said.

"It's cool my nigga, just get us down the way, so that we can get out of this hot ass car."

"Shit!" Bruce said.

"What's wrong?" Dirty asked him.

"I cut my hand." Dirty looked over and seen thick dark blood running down Bruce's hand.

"Damn, you need some stitches for that!"

"I will be all right!" Bruce said and pulled his top shirt off. He tied the shirt around his hand to try and stop the bleeding. George got off of the freeway at the 30th and Woodland exit. He shot up Woodland, and then turned onto Kinsman. He drove over the bridge to the Valley and pulled into the first parking lot. They all hopped out of the car.

"We are going to come back and burn this bitch!" Dirty told them as they took off walking through the Valley.

Ÿ

They walked up the hill to Rab's parking lot and got into Dirty's car. Dirty headed up to Hobo's store. He pulled in front of the store and hopped out with the bag in his hand. He indicated for Bruce to bring his bag and follow him.

They went into Hobo's store, and Dirty were surprised to see Lou behind the counter with Hobo. "I was just about to have Hobo call you for me."

"I'm always a step ahead baby boy! I knew that you would make it happen and I knew that you would come here."

"Let's go into the back so that I can see what y'all got." They went into the back of the store and into the office. Dirty dumped the chains out onto the desk. Lou started to separate them by the type of chains they were, then he started writing the price off of each chain down on a small tablet. The prices on the chains ranged from two hundred to four thousand dollars. There were over twenty chains and Lou used a calculator to tally the price at $96,000.

Lou put the chains back into the bag, and then Bruce took the bricks of rings out of his bags and placed them onto the desk. There were seven bricks of rings, with ten rings in each brick. Only three of the bricks contained rings that had diamonds in them. The other brick had regular gold and nugget rings. Lou tallied the price of all of them at $113,000, and then he added the price of the rings to the price of the chains and came up with the total price of $209,000.

"Well fellas, it all adds up to $209,000. A third of that is $69,666 dollars and 64 cents. My fee is two grand, so that leaves y'all with $67,666 and 64 Cents."

"That's some bullshit!" Bruce yelled.

"Hold up Lou, you ain't say nothing about you getting no fee. You said that you were purchasing the jewelry from us at a third!"

"No I said I was purchasing the stuff from y'all on behalf of someone else at a third."

"This nigga is on some bullshit, he is trying to fuck us Dirty!"

"Dirty, who is this nigga, he ain't even supposed to be here. I'm conducting business with you. Now my fee is coming from me playing the middle man between you and the fence. If you do not like the deal you can always go out there and try to sell it in the streets and take a chance of getting popped off, it's your choice."

Dirty looked at Bruce and said, "Fuck it dawg! It will be better next time!"

"I ain't never fucking with that grimy ass nigga again!" Bruce said to Dirty.

"Give us the money!" Dirty told Lou. Lou left out of the store and went and retrieved a briefcase out the trunk of his car. He reentered the store, laid the case on the desk and popped it open. The brief case was filled with stacks of money.

Lou counted out $69,666 and handed it to Dirty.

"Give us our sixty four cents shiesty ass nigga!" Bruce said to Lou.

"Dirty you need to check your boy, he is starting to get very disrespectful and that ain't healthy."

"What! You threatening me nigga?" Bruce asked Lou getting hype.

"Chill!" Dirty told Bruce realizing that they had to get out of there before the situation escalated.

"Alright Hobo, Alright Lou." Dirty said to them as he started to make his exit.

"We got some more business." Lou said to Dirty.

"No doubt!" Dirty responded, knowing that he was never going to do business with Lou again. He knew in his heart that Lou had played them. Bruce was heated.

Dirty had put him on, so he did not want to cause any trouble for him, but he swore to his self that if he ever saw Lou in the streets that he was going to beat his ass and rob him.

They got into the car and Dirty split up the money. They all got $16,900 apiece. Everybody was fine except for Bruce, "Dirty, you let that fat mother fucker get out on us!"

"Bruce tell me something, have you even seen or had that much money in your life? Come on dawg, just take it as a lesson learned. He put us onto a game, that we can master ourselves. So, we paid to learn how to get some real money. Now let me take you home so that you can put your money up and go to the hospital to get your hand stitched up."

Ÿ

After Dirty dropped Bruce off, he headed over to the west side to his house. When he entered the house he had seen that his Aunt Nita who he couldn't stand was there. Dirty hated her because she got high, was sneaky and always had an attitude. She looked up when he entered, "Boy where your ass been?" she yelled at him.

Dirty ignored her and kept walking towards his room. He went into his room and closed the door. He went over to his nightstand and removed a screwdriver out of the drawer. He used it to unscrew the back of his TV. He removed the back stuffed $16,000 into it then replaced it. He was screwing in the last screw when Nita bust into his room.

"What is you doing?" startled, Dirty dropped the screw driver.

"What the fuck do you want?" Dirty asked her quickly standing up.

"Boy, you are going to stop driving my mother crazy!"

"Nita, who the fuck is you? And why do you keep fucking with me?" Dirty asked her as he grabbed his coat and headed out of the room.

"I know your black ass don't think that you are leaving back out of this house!"

"Your dope fiend ass better beat it!"

"Boy I will beat your ass! You better watch your mouth!"

"Try to put your hand on me if you want, and I swear to you that I will break your fucking jaw!" Dirty told her. She looked Dirty in his eyes and could tell that he was dead serious. She did not say another word as Dirty left the house. Dirty jumped back into his car and headed back over to the east side.

Ÿ

"So what are y'all going to do with your money?" Dirty asked George and Rab.

"I'm going to get me car." George told him.

"What about you Rab?"

"Man, I'm just stacking right now. I might buy me some clothes and a few pair of shoes that's it."

"Nigga you better treat yourself." George told him.

"I might treat my mother to a home makeover, or even move her out of the projects."

"Now that's what's up!" Dirty told him.

"Take care of moms!" he emphasized.

A week had passed and all four of them Dirty, Rab, George and Bruce had spent some of the money that they had gotten from the lick. George had gotten one of his older cousins to put a car in his name. Dirty took him to Rick's trading post, where George copped a 1981 Ninety Eight Regency. It was silver and had leather seats in it. George paid $3,000 for it. He went down to Safeway and had his car fitted with 30's and vogues. He then went to an electronic shop bought and had installed a Jesen stereo system that included an equalizer. After George spending spree he had only $2,000 left from the lick.

Rab bought his mother a $1,000 kitchen set, a $2,000 living room set and a $2,000 dollar bedroom set. He bought his self a $5,000 bedroom set that had a waterbed. He also spent 3,000 dollars buying a 27" color television, a VCR and a stereo system. He also bought his sister Poochie a bedroom set and some clothes. Last he had the apartment cleaned and painted, which got rid of that horrible smell that had been stuck inside of the house for years. Rab still had money from their first lick, so even after his spending spree he still had $4,000 put up.

Bruce was eighteen and he bought a car putting it in his name. He bought a 1980 Caprice Classic. It was a four door that was blue and had metallic flakes inside of the paint. He paid $8,500 for it. He gave China man and Keith each $2,000. After that he had $3,500 dollars left to his name.

Dirty spent the less out of everybody, being that he already had a car. He made sure that he paid Donny off, giving him a thousand dollars. He bought himself and Robin pagers. He also took Robin shopping, getting her a couple of outfits and a pair of shoes. He tried to pick Robin up from school every day. He was still fucking Tonya, but not as much since he started becoming attached to Robin. He did give her a couple hundred dollars.

Tonya was grown and had her own place. Dirty kept in mind that he might need her one day, so he didn't totally cut her off. Dirty was a smart thinker. He never wanted to be on anyone's bad side, because he knew that there was no telling when he would need a favor from someone.

Ÿ

Tim and Ron were at the 40th and Woodland bus stop, waiting to hit a lick. That day, Mike wasn't with them because he had gone with his family to see his older brother who was locked up in Mansfield prison. Tim and Ron pockets were on empty, so they set out to put some money into them. Their flaw was that neither one of them were a thinker or a leader. To them all licks were good licks. They did not know how to distinguish between a good or bad luck.

It was two in the afternoon and it was very hot that day. They appreciated the little bit of shade that the bus shelter was providing for them, it kept the hot sun from beaming down on them directly.

"Man, let's do this. it's hot as hell out here!" Tim told Ronald.

"Fuck it, the next car that stops, I'm hitting it!" Ronald said. Seconds later the light turned red and a Buick Century pulled to a stop at the light. There was an old black lady driving. Ronald stepped off of the curb, raised his arm and threw the bearing through the passenger's side window.

The shattering of the glass startled the old woman, and her foot smashed down on the glass causing her to run through the red light. She went out into oncoming traffic, and her car was slammed into by a pickup truck. The truck hit her on the driver's side.

"Oh Shit!" Ronald said, and then took off running with Tim following behind him. The impact smashed in the frame of the car. The old woman, who had a bad heart, instantly went into cardiac arrest and died. She was dead before help could even get to her.

The driver of the pickup truck was seriously injured. He had cracked his chest plate on the steering wheel. The collision had stopped traffic, and people were exiting their cars to try and help the injured people.

A lady that had been sitting in her window at the time of the incident had witnessed the whole thing. She saw what had caused the accident. She had observed them same boys do what they had done many times before, but never said anything, because the victims usually drove off, never to be seen again. This time was different, people were hurt. After she made sure that she had seen the direction that the boys had run in. She called the police and the paramedics, and then she left her house and went downstairs. There was a huge crowd, and the street was full of people.

The lady, whose name was Ms. Watson walked through the crowd chanting, "I seen it all, I seen what them boys did!" People just looked at her wondering what she was talking about. She was trying to tell anyone who would listen to her what she had seen.

Ÿ

Ron and Tim were up in Ron's house scared to death, "Ain't no shit like that ever happened before!" Ron stated.

"Yeah that shit was crazy!" replied Tim.

"Go back around there and see what's going on." Ron told Tim.

"Nigga is you crazy! I ain't going back to the scene of a crime and get myself knocked off."

"Nigga you ain't did shit, ain't nobody seen you do shit. Just go back around there and see if the lady is okay, then come right back."

"I'm telling you man, shit better not happen to me. I'm going to go around there right quick, but I don't want to do the shit!" Tim said as he headed for the door.

He left out of the project building and walked back around the corner. As he approached Woodland he had seen that a massive crowd had formed. He heard sirens blaring as they reached the scene. Tim made his way closer trying to get a better look. The police were trying to move the crowd back to make room so that the paramedics could tend to the victims.

The Jaws of Life had to be brought to the scene to get the old woman out of her car. When the paramedics got her out of the car and placed her on a gurney, Tim pushed forward trying to get a good look at her. He wanted to see how she was doing. He was unaware that Ms. Watson had witnessed the whole thing from her project window and was in the middle of the crowd talking to the police. When Tim pushed to the front of the crowd, he heard someone yell, "That's one of them right there. Tim looked up and seen an old lady pointing in his direction. Tim quickly turned around and started pushing his way back through the crowd "Hey stop!" an officer yelled after him. Tim started pushing people out of his way, trying to get into the clear, so that he could take off. The police were pursuing him, "Stop!" they yelled as they chased him. Two bystanders had seen Tim coming their way with officers running behind him. When Tim tried to pass them, they each grabbed a hold of him, "Get the fuck off of me!" Tim yelled at the two men as he tussled with them trying to break free. He finally got one of his arms free and used it to hit one of the men on his chin. The man went down and Tim started swinging that same hand at the other man. He caught him two times in the face, before a police officer clobbered him in the back of his head with a baton. The officer hit him repeatedly until he crumbled to the ground. The other officer put his knee in Tim's back and cuffed him.

"I didn't do anything!" Tim yelled as the officers lifted him up and escorted him to their cruiser.

They placed him into the backseat, then went and got Ms. Watson and took her back to their car, so that she could get an up close look at him.

"Is this one of the guys?" one of the officers asked her.

"Yeah he was the look out. It usually be three of them, but this time it was just him and another fella!"

"And what exactly is it that they do?"

"They wait for a car to stop at the red light, then run up on the car and bust the window out."

"What do they use to bust the window out with ma'am?"

"I don't know, but whatever it be it's as small as a rock." she told them.

The officers pulled Tim back out of the car and searched his pockets.

In his front right pocket they found a handful of something that they thought were pellets.

"This must be what she is talking about." one officer said to the other.

"All we got to do is have the CSI Unit sweep the car and see if they find one of these and if they do case solved."

"This fella is either going to give up his partner or take the ride by his self."

They put Tim back into the car and headed downtown to the station. One of the little young cats from Case Court, seen Tim gets put into the police car. He ran to Ron's apartment and knocked on the door. Ron quickly opened the door thinking that it was Tim returning.

"Nigga where you been?" Ron was saying as he opened the door. He was shocked to see that it wasn't Tim at the door, but a little kid that he always seen hanging out.

"The police took your friend."

"They took him for what?"

"Some old lady pointed him out and the police got him. They put him in the back of their car and drove off."

"Shit! Thanks little man!" Ron told him then closed his door.

Ron started pacing back and forth wondering what could have happened. He couldn't understand how or why they had taken Tim. The old lady that pointed Tim out must have seen them he thought. He figured that he needed to lay low until he heard from Tim.

Tim was downtown in an interview room inside of the homicide unit. Detectives Parker and Mitchell entered the room.

Detective Parker held in his hand a plastic baggie that contained one of the bearings. He sat the bag down on the conference table as he sat down, Mitchell remained standing.

"Timothy Barnes is your name right?" detective Parker asked him.

"Yeah that's it."

"Okay, so where is your friend that threw the pellet through the old lady's window?"

"I don't know what you are talking about. I don't even know why I am down here."

"Mr. Barnes, you can play dumb all you want, but let me explain something to you, that lady died. The person that was in the other vehicle is in critical condition. Now we have a witness that identified you. You were found with a pocket full of pellets, and we retrieved one of those pellets from the lady's car. I don't know if you know this, but an accomplice can be charged with the same type of charge as the perpetrator. So if you want to face an aggravated murder and robbery charge all by yourself be my guess, I promise you that if you don't give your partner up, that I am going to personally see to it that you get buried under the jail. Now you let that marinate in your brain for a few minutes, then I will be back to talk to you again." Parker rose up out of his seat and headed out of the room, with Mitchell following behind him.

"You think he's going to break?" Mitchell asked Parker.

"If he has any sense he will. I'm going to grab me a cup of coffee right quick." Parker told Mitchell as he headed down the hall to the break room.

When he got back from the break room, detective Mitchell was standing there talking to a middle aged black woman. Mitchell looked up when he seen Parker approaching, "Ray this is Mrs. Barnes, she is Timothy's mother."

"How are you doing Mrs. Barnes?" Parker said to her as he extended his hand for her to shake.

"What are y'all holding my boy for?" she asked them.

"Please step into our conference room and we will explain." Parker told her.

She followed them into a conference room and they explained the circumstances to her.

"So, it wasn't him that did it?" she asked them to confirm that he did not cause the lady's death.

"No he was an accomplice to the person that actually did it. And as I explained to him Mrs. Barnes, an accomplice can be held to the same level of responsibility as the actual perpetrator. So if we do not find his accomplice he will take the fall all by his self." Parker told her.

"Can I talk to him please?" she asked the officers.

"Sure, hopefully you can convince him to do the right thing, follow us please." Parker and Mitchell led her over to the interview room that Tim was being held in. They opened the door and stepped in. Tim looked up and was surprised to see his mother step into the room with the officers.

"Timothy dammit! What's going on?"

"I don't know these police just jumped on me and brung me down here."

"They ain't just brung your ass down here for nothing, now who was with you?"

"Wasn't no one with me, because I didn't do nothing?"

"Detective could I talk to him in private for a minute?"

"Sure!" said detective Parker. Him and Mitchell stepped out and went into the adjoining next room that had a one way mirror and was equipped to listen to everything that was said in the other room. Tim's mother sat down in a chair. Tears started to form in the corner of her eyes. Ever since her husband had died her son had begun hanging with the wrong crowd and started to get in trouble. He was sixteen years old sitting up in the homicide division.

"Tim, they say that they are going to charge you with murder if you don't tell them who was with you. I lost your dad, I ain't trying to lose you too. Just tell the people what they want to know baby."

"I ain't telling them crackers shit! I ain't giving up my boy!"

"Your boy!"

"Is you stupid are you willing to spend the rest of your life in jail for your boy?"

"I'm a juvenile, I will get out by the time I'm twenty one."

"When did you become so cold? How did you become so lost? I did everything that I could for you, why are you like this?"

"Ma, I ain't trying to hear all of that. You can stop the crying and go on home!" Tim told her as he folded his arms across his chest and leaned back in his chair. After Parker and Mitchell heard the last part of their conversation, they decided to step back into the room. They left out of the adjoining room and reentered the interview room.

"Mrs. Barnes could we talk to you for a second please?" Parker asked her. They stepped out into the hall.

"Mrs. Barnes we heard your conversation. It is evident that he isn't going to talk, so we have to book him, and then send him over to juvenile hall. Do you know any of his friends that he hangs with? You helping us may, could also help him."

"I just know two of the boy's name that he hangs around. One name is Ronald, I think his last name is Greene, but I'm not sure. The other one I only know him as Mike."

"Thank you for your time and help Mrs. Barnes. I know how hard this must be for you. I have kids too, and us as parents try to do all that we can to keep our children on the right track. Sometimes that's just not enough, so don't you go harboring the blame for what Timothy has done." Parker told her.

"When will I be able to see him?"

"You should be able to visit him down at juvenile hall tomorrow." Parker told her as he led her out front.

When he went back into his office, he told Mitchell to run a check on the name Ronald Greene and see if he could get a picture of him.

Chapter 12

Bruce was up in the plaza shooting dice. Since he had hit the jewelry lick, he had been stunting like he was a dope boy. He had been riding around with a knot of money on him splurging.

When he got down to only fifteen hundred left, he figured that he needed to flip it. He decided that the best way to do that was to shoot dice.

Bruce was an amateur for real. Most of his winnings came from luck. He decided to shoot against little Vic, who was a professional.

Little Vic was one of the few people that could turn gambling into a hustle. Whatever he chose to gamble in he made sure that the odds were in his favor, by knowing and being able to do something extra.

When it came to playing cards, Vic knew how to read the cards, read the people that he was playing cards against. He also knew how to count the cards and set the deck on his deal. When it came to shooting dice, he knew how to set them, how to pad roll them and how to switch out good dice with loaded dice.

Everyone in the neighborhood knew that, Vic rarely lost. Vic had won cars from shooting dice. For some reason Bruce thought that he could take him. He called Vic out, "What's up old drunk ass nigga, you trying to get broke?"

"Youngster, you better take your big mouth, big lip ass back over to Green Court before you end up walking back over there dead broke!"

"Nigga you can't break me! What the hit for?"

"Alright youngster, I'm going to give you what you're looking for." Vic told him.

"We are going to roll one dice to see who shoots first." Bruce told him.

"Whatever!" Bruce rolled one dice, and it stopped on the number five. Next Vic rolled the dice and it stopped on the number three.

Vic shot first and the dice never made it to Bruce. Vic hit every point that he rolled. All Bruce was left with was ten dollars to his name.

"What's up young blood? I know you ain't broke that fast!" Vic said to him when he seen that Bruce did not have any more money in his hand.

"Nigga I ain't broke! I just don't have any more money on me."

"Shit! You got that pretty ass car. I will put seven grand up against it." Bruce thought about it. He knew that Vic had the hot hand, but he thought that if he got a chance to shoot, the dice, that he could win his money back. He thought that if worst came to worst little Vic couldn't beat him fighting and he wasn't no killer, so if he lost he ain't have to pay him.

"Let me shoot first and you got a bet!" Bruce told Vic.

"Let's get this straight, you are really shooting on ass, so if you go down and quit before we reach seven thousand I hold onto the car until you bring me the money. If you lose the whole seven thousand then the car is mine. Do we have an understanding?"

"I hear all that you are saying, but I don't plan on losing." Vic turned to the crowd of spectators that had gathered to watch them shoot.

"Now y'all witnessed this. He is putting his car up against seven thousand dollars, and he is shooting first!"

"We heard him!" said some of the spectators.

"Nigga, this ain't no courtroom. We don't need no fucking witnesses, let's go." The crowd of spectators formed a circle around them.

Bruce held the dice, "We ain't shooting for no little money. The game will take all day, so let's shoot for five hundred a pop!" Vic told Bruce.

"Nigga shoot a thousand!" Bruce said getting cocky.

"Have it your way, shoot the dice."

Bruce shook the dice and rolled them. They stopped on a five and a three making his point eight. "A thousand say you don't six eight" Vic said to Bruce.

"Nigga bet!" Bruce said as he shook the dice and rolled them. They landed on six, one he had crapped out. He was down two thousand dollars.

He picked the dice up and blew on them, "Come on baby help me break this lame!" Bruce said to the dice before he shot them. They landed on double six, he crapped out. "Shit!" he said to his self as he picked the dice back up. He rolled them, again and crapped out for the third straight time. Within two minutes Bruce was down four thousand dollars. The crowd started egging him on. Some jeered him, calling him slept rock and telling him that he needed a lucky charm. Bruce loved to talk shit but he couldn't stand for anyone to talk shit back to him. He yelled to the crowd, "I know y'all want to see me lose to this old fool, but I'm about to take this nigga to school and beat him out of his shoes. When I get through roasting this nigga like a duck anyone of you broke mother fuckers can press your luck." The crowd got riled up while Vic just stood there smiling, "Fuck all that extra shit young blood, shoot the dice!" Vic told him.

"Here they come, you MD 20/20 drinking ass nigga!" Bruce said as he rolled the dice. He rolled a ten. "Bet a thousand you don't ten or four?" Vic said to him.

"No bet!" Bruce rolled the dice and hit his point. He instantly wishes he had taken the side bet. He rolled again and hit craps. He was down only two thousand. He had won two bets in a row. He thought he was getting hot.

"Double the bet nigga!" he told Vic.

"Bet!" Bruce rolled the dice and got eight as his point.

"A thousand you don't six or eight!" Vic said to him.

"Bet!" Bruce rolled the dice three times, before he crapped out. He was back down five thousand.

"Fuck it, shoot the last two!" Bruce said.

"Go ahead and shoot yourself out." Bruce shook the dice for about a minute before he shot them. He held his breath and closed his eyes for a moment. For the moment that he had his eyes closed he prayed that he hit. He opened his eyes as the dice tumbled they both landed on snake eyes, and Bruce had lost again. The crowd broke out laughing, "Pass the keys young one!" Vic said to Bruce.

"Fuck you nigga! Get them like Ali got the title." Someone from the crowd yelled, "Sore loser!" Bruce replied, "Fuck all you bitches!" then strutted to his car, "This time you, next time me young blood!" Vic said to Bruce as he jumped into his car and pulled off.

Two dudes stepped out of the crowd and approached Vic. One of them spoke, "Five hundred and we will burn that car to a crisp."

"Make it like Bar-B-Que and I got y'all."

"Enough said!" replied the man, then him and his partner walked off.

Ÿ

Bruce headed up to the court to get China man and Keith. When he got up there, they were standing on the sideline waiting on winners.

He blew his horn, they looked up and he waved them over. They walked towards his car. When they got there China Man asked him, "Nigga, where you been?"

"1 was up in the Plaza shooting dice with that nigga Vic."

"Vic nigga! You shot against Vic, I know you're broke."

"How the fuck you figure that?"

"Cause the nigga Vic don't lose. He be winning cars from niggas and shit. You lucky you still driving."

"Nigga you got me fucked up. I only lost a couple hundred to the nig-ga." Bruce wasn't going to tell him the truth that he had actually lost all of his money and his car, but that he bucked on that bet. "Get in, we are going downtown to check out a lick I want to hit tomorrow."

"What kind of lick?" China Man asked him.

"Nigga you are full of questions today. What you are playing Perry Mason?"

"Fuck you nigga! I just like to know what I'm getting into. I ain't no flunky or fool ass nigga that just do anything."

"We are going to hit a jewelry lick nigga, you satisfied?"

"What! The nigga Dirty is putting us on?"

"Nigga, fuck Dirty! We are doing this ourselves. All we need is a couple hammers and a getaway car."

"Shit, holla at Mike. He know how to steal cars, plus he might want to get in on the lick." Keith told Bruce. Bruce thought about it, and realized that it did take four people. He called over to the court for Mike, who had been hanging solo ever since Tim had gotten arrested and Ron was in hiding.

Mike walked over to them, "What's up Bruce?"

"We are about to hit a jewelry lick tomorrow, and we need you to steal us a car, plus you can go with us on the lick if you want."

"What! Y'all are going to rob the store with a gun?" he asked them pulling out a small twenty two pistol.

"Nigga put that shit up, we ain't using no guns. We are going to use hammers to bust the cases and snatch the jewelry."

"You are going to walk into a jewelry store with some big ass hammers."

"You got a better idea?" Bruce asked him. Mike reached into his pocket and pulled out a bearing.

"All we need is these." he said showing them the bearing.

"Man, I ain't got no time to see if that little mother fucker works. You can use it, but I'm going with what I know works. Anyway we are about to go and scope the store out right quick. We need you to go and find a car."

"Take me with y'all and I will get a car to bring back."

"Alright, get in." Bruce told him.

Bruce headed downtown, because it was closer he thought that it would be easier to hit a lick and get away. Bruce did not have the same type of thinking and planning skills that Dirty had. His idea of planning was just to find a store and hit it.

They got downtown, parked and got out of the car. Mike walked off from them. Bruce and his boys walked halfway down the block to the

Euclid Arcade. They entered the Arcade, which had a number of stores inside of it. Two of the stores just happened to be jewelry stores.

Roger's jewelry store had a big picture window that allowed you to view the whole store from the outside. Bruce looked through the window and seen an older looking Italian man. He thought to his self, "This is it." He turned to his boys, "Alright lets go." They went back to his car.

Bruce drove to a hardware store and told Keith, "Give me twenty dollars."

"Fuck is your money at?"

"I ain't got it on me, now give me twenty fucking dollars, so that I can buy some damn hammers!" Keith gave Bruce twenty dollars and he went into the store and bought three hammers. He jumped back in the car and drove back down the way. When he pulled up to the basketball court, Mike was already there sitting on the hood of a four door Chevy Cavalier.

"What took y'all so long." he said smiling.

"Nigga, drive that car to my lot and I'm going to follow you. We got to park it so don't shit happen to it." Bruce told him. Mike jumped into the car and pulled off with Brace following him.

Chapter 13

Dirty had not been home in a couple of days. He had been spending the night at Tonya's house. He had gotten low on money and decided to head home to get some more money out of his stash. When he got to the house, his grandma Pearl was sitting in the kitchen. He walked over to her and gave her a hug, "Hey granny."

"Boy, don't you be hey grannying me. I have been sitting here worried sick about you. I do got a phone you know. You can call me from time to time when you out running them streets to let me know that you are okay!"

"You are right, I promise from here on out I'm going to call you and check in with you." Dirty told her then headed down the hall to his room. When he entered his room, he got a funny feeling. He walked over to his television set and noticed that the back of it was loosely hanging off. He instantly reflected back to his aunt Nita busting into his room when he was putting the back of the TV back on.

He looked down and seen two screws and the screwdriver lying on the floor. He picked the screwdriver up and removed the two screws that were loosely holding the back on. He knew before he took the back off that his money wasn't going to be there.

"I'm going to kill that bitch!" he said to his self.

Dirty was usually laid back and he rarely ever got angry, but his blood started to boil, he had never had anything taken from him before. "This must be Karma," he thought to his self. Someone was showing him how the people that he took from felt when they had their things taken from them.

Dirty stormed back up to the front room and scared his grandmother when he yelled at her "Pearl! Who been here?" startled she looked at him and seen the crazed look on his face, "What do you mean who been here Tyrone? What's wrong?"

"Who has been in this house in the last couple of days?"

"Ain't nobody been here, but me and Nita." There it was, Dirty had his confirmation. He turned and headed back down the hall.

"What's wrong Tyrone?" his grandmother yelled after him.

"Don't worry about it!" he yelled back as he entered his room and slammed the door.

Dirty sat on his bed and pulled out a wet stick that was wrapped in aluminum foil. He lit the joint and started taking deep pulls. The wet was so potent that he was only able to smoke a quarter of it. He put the rest of it out and sat there in a zone. He got up and went into the living room and sat in a reclining chair that faced the door. He sat there in that spot for over three hours. His grandmother had gone to bed.

It was about eleven o'clock, when Dirty heard a key in the door. He quickly jumped up ran into the kitchen grabbed a frying pan out of the dish rack and ducked down behind the counter.

Nita entered the house. She was high from being on a three day binge. She had spent about two thousand dollars in three days getting high, plus she had splurged another two thousand, just giving money away to her smoker friends and the lady that ran the house that they all got high over. She had almost twelve thousand dollars wrapped in a bandanna, stuffed inside of her panties. She had not eaten or showered in three days. She was hungry and went into the kitchen to get something to eat.

She headed to the refrigerator, opened it, and bent over to look inside to see what Ms. Pearl had to eat. Dirty stood up and crept up behind her and as soon as she stood up straight, Dirty cracked her in the back of her head with the frying pan.

"You go steal from me, you dope fiend bitch!"

"Tyrone stop! Ma help!" Nita yelled as she tried to get away from Dirty.

Dirty grabbed her by the back of her shirt and snatched her back to him, "Where my money bitch? You ain't smoked it all." Dirty said to her then cracked her in her back with the pan. Nita crumbled to the floor. Dirty dropped the pan and dropped to the floor with her and began raining punches down on her.

"Tyrone! Tyrone you stop that!" Ms. Pearl yelled at him from the kitchen doorway.

"This bitch took my money granny, tell her to give me my shit." Dirty said to Ms. Pearl as he hit Nita in her face.

"Nita please baby give him his money! Just give it to him!"

"Okay! Okay just tell him to get off of me."

"Tyrone she is going to give you the money, now let her up!" Dirty got up but still stood over top of Nita, who unbuttoned her pants and pulled the bandanna full of money out of it, "Here boy!" she said to Dirty, handing the bandanna to him.

Dirty still mad about what she had done drew his leg back and kicked her so hard in her chest that Ms. Pearl thought for sure that he had broken some bones.

"Dammit Tyrone you got your money now leave her alone before I call the police." Dirty stuffed the bandanna into his pocket and headed for the door. He stopped at the door, turned around and said, "You lucky bitch! If you ever take anything from me again, I will kill you."

Nita laid curled up on the kitchen floor moaning. Ms. Pearl ran to the telephone to call the paramedics. She was praying that Nita was going to be alright. Dirty jumped into his car and headed over to Tonya's house. When he got there, Tonya was sitting up in her bedroom crying.

When Dirty entered her room he smelled PCP, "This bitch tripping off of wet!" Dirty thought to his self.

"Who is Robin Dirty?" Tonya asked him crying.

"Fuck is you talking about?"

"Don't play with me nigga!" Tonya told him, and then pulled a butcher's knife from underneath her pillow.

"Tonya you better stop tripping. If you can't handle smoking wet leave that shit alone." Tonya stood up from the bed.

"I ain't the one tripping nigga! You playing me for a little high school bitch. Do she fuck you better than I do? Do she suck your dick better than I do huh? You got me fucked up, I ain't no punk!" she said and then lunged at Dirty with the knife raised.

Dirty side stepped her and grabbed her arm. He twisted her arm until she dropped the knife out of her hand. He then put her into a choke hold until she collapsed to the floor sitting Indian style. Bubbles started forming at the corner of her mouth as she struggled to breathe, "I'm pregnant Dirty!" she whispered. Dirty loosened his grip on her throat, "What did you say bitch?"

"I'm pregnant! You are going to make me lose my baby!"

"Bitch! You should of thought about of that before your dumb ass pulled a knife on me!" he told her. Dirty knew that he was probably already in trouble for what he had done to Nita. He did not want to be in any more trouble than he was probably already in, so he let her go.

She laid there on the floor crying and trying to catch her breath. Dirty was tired, but decided that he could not stay at Tonya's that night. She had pulled a knife on him. He figured that he could not trust her, so he left.

As he was leaving Tonya yelled out, "I love you!" after him. Dirty left out of her house, jumped into his car and drove up to Rab's house. Rab let him in and seen the look on Dirty's face.

"What's wrong dawg?"

"Bitches are crazy, I need some sleep." he followed him into his bedroom where he found himself a place on the floor laid down and crashed.

Chapter 14

Bruce, China Man and Keith left out of Bruce's house early the next morning heading out to the parking lot. Soon as they got outside of the building a strong, strange smell of something burning hit their noses, "Fuck is that burning?" Keith asked to no one in particular.

"It smells like rubber and some other shit!" China Man said as they walked around the building to the parking lot. As soon as they turned the corner, they all had seen thick, dark smoke coming from a smoldering can.

It took Bruce a minute for him to register that it was his car that had been burned to a crisp.

"Damn!" China Man said.

"I'm going to kill that nigga!" Bruce said as he walked over to what used to be his car. The car was only a shell. There was no longer any interior left in the car. The tires of the car had burned and melted. The heat from the burning car had warped the spokes of his whale rims.

"You know who did this?" China Man asked him.

"It don't matter, I will deal with this later, let's go." They all got into the stolen Cavalier, with Bruce driving. He drove over to Case Court and pulled in front of Mike's row house and blew the horn. Mike opened the door, stepped out and shut the door behind him. He went to the car and got into the back seat.

Bruce took off, "What's up with y'all?" Mike asked them. They all remained quiet. Mike thought that perhaps they were just getting mentally psyched up to hit the lick, so he just sat back and remained quiet also.

When they got downtown Bruce found a parking spot that was almost right in front of the Arcade. He put the car in park, "Keith, you get over here in the driver's seat and stay ready. China you stay out in the hallway and watch out for D.D.A. Mike you coming in with me." Bruce grabbed a hammer from under the seat and said, "Let's go!"

Him, China Man and Mike got out of the car and walked into the Arcade. Bruce and Mike headed into Roger's jewelry store, while China Man roamed the corridor of the Arcade.

When they entered the store, the old Italian man looked up and seen that it was two young black guys and he hit a button under the counter that automatically locked the door. They were locked inside of the store and did not even know it. The old man did not trust blacks, especially young ones.

Bruce and Mike separated when they entered the store. Bruce approached the man, while Mike stopped at a counter that contained watches. Some were gold, some were stainless steel and some were platinum. Bruce spoke to the old man, "How are you doing sir?" The old man with a mean straight face asked him, "What can I help you with?"

Bruce took notice of the man's attitude. "I'm trying to buy a chain." Bruce told him, looking at the chains inside of the display case.

"How much are you trying to spend?" asked the old man.

"About a thousand dollars." The old man looked at the way Bruce was dressed and could not see him having a thousand dollars to spend on a chain.

"Do you have a thousand dollars on you?"

"Do you treat all of your customers like this?" Bruce asked him getting angry.

"If you do not have any money, you can leave my store!" Mike was getting tired of the back and forth that was going on between Bruce and the old man. He pulled a bearing out of his pocket and smashed the case that he was standing in front of.

The shattering of the glass caused both Bruce and the old man to look towards Mike who was snatching watches out of the case and stuffing them into his pockets, "You damn nigger!" the old man yelled at Mike as he ran towards him. Bruce pulled the hammer from his waist and busted the display case in front of him. The old man turned back around and seen Bruce snatching jewelry out of the other case.

"I got something for you niggers!" The old man said as he took off running into a backroom of the store. They thought that he was going to call the police.

"Let's go Bruce yelled to Mike." Mike, who was closer to the door, took off towards it. Once he got to it he tried to pull it open but it wouldn't budge.

"Open that mother fucker!" yelled Bruce. Mike put both of his hands on the door and tried to open it.

"Shit! It's locked, it won't open!" Mike told him.

"He must of hit a switch behind the counter!" Bruce said as he turned and headed towards the counter. Right when Bruce got to the counter the old man reappeared from the back holding a twelve gauge shotgun.

"You son of a bitches!" the man yelled then started unloading buck shots. Bruce fell on the floor on the other side of the counter out of the line of fire. The man fired at Mike who was by the door. When Mike seen he raised the shot gun in his direction he dove behind another display case. He hit the floor and pulled his twenty two out of his pocket and returned fire. The old man was shocked when Mike started firing back. He backed up towards the backroom letting off a wild shot that shattered the glass in the door.

Mike saw the glass in the door shatter making an escape route. He stood up quickly and let off another shot that struck the old man in the shoulder.

The old man slid down the wall, and Mike took off running through the empty space in the door. Bruce jumped up and followed him.

China Man was standing at the entrance to the Arcade. When he heard the shots being fired, he bolted because people had started coming out of the stores to see what was going on. He was the first one to make it to the car. Many people stood in the corridor, watching Bruce and Mike make a getaway.

An employee from another store followed them and watched them jump into the car and pull off. The employee ran back into the store and called the police giving them a description of the car.

It was a business day and the traffic downtown was heavy. Keith weaved in and out of traffic trying to get away, but traffic kept stopping. When they got to 9th and Prospect there was a motorcycle cop directing traffic, because one of the lanes was shut down being worked on.

They heard sirens in the distance, "Fuck that! Go!" Bruce yelled to Keith. Keith pulled around the car that was in front of him and shot through the light almost hitting the motorcycle cop. A car that had the right away clipped the back end of the Cavalier, almost sending them into a spin.

Keith straightened the car out and took off. The motorcycle cop radioed in for back up then gave chase. Keith kept blowing the car's horn, trying to get the cars that were in front of him to get out of his way.

A police car that was coming in the opposite direction from them, turned sideways and stopped, trying to cut them off.

Keith made a sharp right turn onto a side street and found himself on a one way street with traffic coming in the opposite direction. There were two lanes of oncoming traffic, coming directly at them.

The oncoming cars blew their horns and swerved in order to prevent from having a head on collision with them.

China Man and Mike were crouched down in the back seat bracing themselves for the crash that they knew they were bound to have.

"Get on the sidewalk!" Bruce told Keith. Keith made another hard right to prevent from hitting an oncoming car then jumped onto the sidewalk. He had the car doing almost sixty miles per hour, driving on the sidewalk.

When they came to the entrance of the one way street, police cars were coming from every direction. They were only two blocks away from the 30th projects.

"Just get to the jets and we are alright!" Bruce yelled. Keith pushed down harder on the gas pedal, driving at seventy five miles per hour through the city's streets.

He was approaching an intersection and the light was red. Traffic that had the right away was moving fast. Keith knew that he did not have a possible chance of making it through without causing an accident, but he still pushed down harder on the gas. Bruce put both of his hands on the dashboard to brace himself. Keith made it halfway through the intersection before the back end of the car got clipped again. The small Cavalier was hit by a van that sent the car into a spin. The four boys that were inside of the car felt like they were on some type of ride at an amusement park as the car kept spinning. The car spinning out of control went up onto the sidewalk and hit a fire hydrant. Bruce quickly jumped out of the car. The bag in his hand got caught by the door latch and ripped. Gold chains started falling out of the hole in the bag. He had no time to stop to get the falling chains.

He clutched the bag trying to prevent any more chains from falling. Mike was right, on his heels as he headed for the projects. The driver's side of the car had hit the hydrant and the frame of the car had been dented in. Neither driver's side door worked. China Man crawled over to the passenger's side of the car, got out and took off running after Bruce and Mike. Keith was the only one that could not escape. His legs were pinned underneath the dashboard. By the time the police had reached the scene, he was the only one left to be apprehended. Bruce, Mike and China Man had all gotten away, running into the 30th housing projects where they found shelter over a girl's house that Bruce knew.

Chapter 15

Detectives Parker and Mitchell were in their car heading to see Ms. Watson. They had a picture of Ronald Greene.

Mitchell had ran him through the system and found out that he had numerous arrest, with some including robbery. He printed a picture of Ronald Greene out. He wanted to show it to Ms. Watson, to see if she would identify him as the assailant.

When they got to her house, she was posted up in her usual spot, her window. She watched the detectives park and exits their car. She seen them heading in the direction of her house and decided to go and meet them at the door. Parker raises his hand to knock, but before he could the door flew open startling him. He took a step back, and Ms. Watson appeared in the door way smiling, "How are you doing officers?"

"We are just fine Ms. Watson." Parker told her as he let out a deep breath.

"Would you like to come in?"

"We would be very grateful." Ms. Watson cleared the doorway and allowed them to enter "Would y'all like to have a seat?"

"That's okay, this shouldn't take long. We just want to show you a picture to see if you can identify someone for us." Parker told her as he pulled a photo out of his jacket pocket. He handed the photo to Ms. Watson, "Do you recognize him?" Parker asked her.

"This here is that other fella. This is the one that threw whatever it was through that poor woman's car window."

"Are you sure that is him?" Parker asked her again wanting to make sure that she was positive.

"Yes, that is him! I done seen him enough times to know who he is. He stays right around the corner somewhere." Parker knew then that she was sure, because the address that they had on him was right around the corner from Ms. Watson's house.

"Ms. Watson once we have him in custody, we will need you to come down to the station to pick him out of a lineup, is that okay?"

"Anything to get them hoodlums off of the streets. Y'all just have to come and get me, because I do not have a car and my bus pass has expired."

"Don't worry, we will come and get you. Once again thanks for your time and your help." Parker told her as he made his exit.

Ms. Watson followed them to the door and stood in her screen door and watched them get into their car and pull off.

Parker drove right around the corner to Case Court. He pulled over, parked two buildings over from Ronald's, "This isn't the building." Mitchell told him reading the address on the building.

"I know, I say we do a little stake out first. If we go to his home and someone answers but he is not there they are going to warn him that we are looking for him and he might flee. We are going to sit here until we get a visual on him then apprehend him."

"Sounds like a plan." Mitchell said then sat back getting comfortable.

They sat in their car for over two and a half hours before they finally got a break. Ronald appeared in the buildings doorway, looked both ways making sure that the close was clear then stepped out of the building with his arm draped around a girl's shoulder and headed down the street.

"That's him right there." Parker said to Mitchell.

"I'm going to go after him on foot and you pull down in front of him." Mitchell told Parker opening the car door.

"Wait for me to get in front of him before you make a move." Parker told him then started the car and pulled off.

Mitchell went into a light jog trying to catch up to Ronald and the girl. Parker drove down the street past them and pulled over. He was driving a ford LTD which could pass for a detective's car, but Ronald paid it no mind when it drove by. Mitchell was then only a few feet behind him, with his gun drawn and at his side.

Parker pulled over, parked and pulled the lever that opens the car's hood. He stepped out of the car, went to the front of it and lifted the car's hood up. He pretended to be working on the car. He drew his pistol and waited.

As soon as Ronald and the girl were beside the car he stepped out in front of them, with his gun pointing at them, "Ronald Greene!"

Ron looked up, withdrew his arm from the girl and pushed her towards Parker. He turned around preparing to run the other way, but to his surprise Mitchell was standing there with a gun pointed at the middle of his chest, "Ronald Greene we have a warrant for your arrest, please put your hands on the top of your head." Ronald with a look of defeat on his face obeyed. Parker stepped up behind him, putting one hand at a time behind his back and cuffing him. They escorted him back to their car and put him in the back seat.

The first thing that came to Ronald's mind was that Tim had given him up. When they got him down to the station, they took him into the interview room hoping to get a confession out if him. Parker knew that they had enough on him, but felt that it was always best to get the suspect to admit to the crime themselves.

So they set out to get a confession, "Well Mr. Greene, I think you know why you are here." Parker said to him.

"No, I do not know why I am here."

"Well, let me refresh your memory. You threw a pellet through an old unsuspecting lady's car window that eventually led to her death, and has a man lying up in the hospital fighting for his life."

"I don't know what you are talking about!"

"You might as well make it light on yourself. You have two witnesses against you and one of them is a very close friend of yours. We just want to hear your side of the story."

"1 don't have a side, because I haven't done anything."

"Okay then, have it your way!" Parker told him. Ronald was booked then transferred to juvenile hall. He was processed in, given a bedroll and taken up to a unit. When he entered the unit all the kids turned around to see who the new kid was, "Ron what's up?" Tim said smiling as he approached him. Ronald dropped the bedroll and headed towards Tim. When he got within reach he stole on Tim, hitting him in his face. Tim was shocked, which caused him to hesitate, allowing Ronald to follow up with another blow to his face.

"You snitching bitch ass nigga!" he yelled at Tim. Tim quickly recovered from the blows. He had Ronald by at least twenty pounds, and when Ronald tried to rush up on him again, he caught him with a blow that put him down on his ass. While he sat there in a daze on the floor, Tim stood over him. "Nigga what the fuck is wrong with you! I ain't no snitch! I bucked on the police and my mother. They threatened to give me a murder charge and they did. Some old bitch that stay on Woodland by the bus stop pointed me out. She probably got you too!"

"They said that they got two witnesses against me and that one of them is a close friend of mine."

"Well it ain't me, plus how you go believe what they say? You think because they are the law that what they say is law? You can't trust them crackers. Nigga we here on the same pod together. We are going to have to go to court together and the truth will come out and you are going to owe me a apology for assassinating my character like that. Now come on over to my bunk so I can give you some munchies."

Ronald followed Tim over to his bunk and sat down. They ate snicker bars and tried to come up with a plan to get out of the trouble that they were in.

Chapter 16

Dirty went over to his uncle Loft's house. Loft was upset with Dirty for putting his hands on his sister and upsetting his mother.

"You ain't have to beat Nita like that. You know she gets high and that you can't leave nothing around her. She is fucked up pretty bad and my mother is still shaking. You can't be doing that shit man! Is you hearing me?"

"Yeah I'm hearing you unc, I been tripping man. I don't know what it is."

"It's that damn water Red. You need to leave that shit alone."

"I can't unc, it's the only way that I can deal with the pain, plus it's my motivation."

"What do you mean it's your motivation?"

"When I smoke that water, it tells me get that money Dirty."

"Nigga you are crazy, what is up though?"

"I need you to get me a house in your name, I already got it hooked up. All you got to do is sign the lease for me and I'm good."

"You see how you come to me in your times of need. Come to me when shit goes wrong too. Like with what happened with Nita. Let me handle it, okay?"

"I got you unc." Loft went with Dirty over to Colfax, a little side street that was across the street from Garden Valley. He signed a lease renting Dirty a single family, two bedroom home. Dirty had fully furnished his new home. He had carpet laid in every room of the house. He bought a bedroom set, a living room set and a kitchen set. He even bought a queen size bed to put in the spare bedroom. He bought a home entertainment center, a VCR and a 32" color television.

After paying the rent up the three months in advance and furnishing the house. Dirty was left with about $2,500. He knew that he would have to hit a lick soon to stay up, but he was happy and felt that it was worth it. Now he had his own spot, and didn't have to hide his shit from nobody, nor did he have to worry about a crazy bitch trying to stab him in his sleep. The plus was that Robin stayed right down the street, so she could stay at his house and make it home anytime that she needed to.

Soon as the movers delivered the furniture he had her put everything in order. She had to call some of her friends to help her.

Dirty had George and Rab help him move all of the heavy stuff for the girls. They loved the fact that their boy had his own spot. It gave them a spot to chill. Robin also had a place to let her friends come and chill with her. She would go home at night and wait for her grandmother to go to sleep then sneak back out of the house and go spend the night with Dirty. Now that they were free to fuck as they pleased, they started experimenting. They rented some pornos watched them then imitated what they seen on them.

Dirty tried his best to eat her pussy as good as the white boy on TV did with his girl, and Robin gave Dirty head, even though her teeth would scrape his dick, Dirty still enjoyed the feeling of having his dick in her mouth.

Sometimes they would fuck all day, and walk around the house naked. Robin only had one problem with Dirty and that was him smoking wet. She felt that when he smoked it, he became withdrawn and closed her out. She was trying to get the courage to confront him about it.

She sat in the house talking to Lynn and fat Monique, "I think I'm pregnant y'all."

"Have you told Dirty?" Lynn asked her.

"No, I ain't tell him, because I don't know if I'm going to keep it."

"Why?"

"I love Red, but he smokes that wet too much and it turns him into a different person."

"Have you talked to him about it?"

"No, because he treats me so good that I don't want him to feel like I am ungrateful."

"Robin, this is serious. You are talking 'bout a baby, fuck how he feels. Y'all need to talk and come to a understanding about the life that you are carrying inside your stomach!"

"She is right, you need to talk to him and tell him how you feel." fat Monique told her. After hearing her girls input, she decided that she would talk to Dirty that night when he came in.

Dirty got in about midnight. Robin was in his bed naked up under the covers, asleep. Dirty sat on the side of the bed and started removing his clothes. He pulled the covers back to climb under them and seen that Robin was naked. Seeing her naked made his dick get rock hard. It didn't matter if he saw Robin ten times naked in one day. His dick would get hard all ten times. That's the type of effect that her body had on him.

He slid in the bed and up behind her. He took one hand and spread her ass cheeks and used his other hand to guide his dick to her pussy, entering her from the back.

Robin's pussy was super wet and hot. Sinking his dick into her pussy was like sinking into a hot tub, it felt so soothing.

Robin became fully awake. She arched her back pushing her ass back on Dirty. She kept her eyes closed and just enjoyed the feeling that she was getting from Dirty fucking her. Dirty nibbled on her ear, then whispered into it, "Ooh, your pussy is so wet, it feels so good," He reached his arms around to the front of her, and cupped her titties.

Robin bit down on her bottom lip. It was like their body was molded together. Robin's back was completely up against Dirty's chest. Every part of their body was touching. They even, had their feet intertwined.

Robin reached her hand behind her and rubbed on Dirty's hand and face. Dirty stuck one of his fingers into her mouth and she sucked on it like a baby sucks on a pacifier. Dirty was about to cum and he told her, "I'm 'bout to bust in you." That only heightened Robin's arousal and she started cumming also. She bit down on Dirty's finger as she came. Their bodies were soaking wet.

Dirty just held onto her tightly as if he did not want to let her go.

"I'm pregnant Dirty." Hearing those words was like dejavu to Dirty. He let go of her and sat up, "What did you say?"

She sat up also, "I said I am pregnant."

Dirty got a different type of feeling from hearing her say those words than he got when he heard them from Tonya. He felt elated hearing those words come from Robin's mouth.

"I don't know if I'm going to have it though." she told him.

"What do you mean you don't know if you are going to have it?" Dirty asked her then stood up.

"I don't know if you are ready for a baby. You be smoking all that water and it be changing you. I think you might need some type of help."

"Robin, have I ever did wrong by you?"

"No!"

"Have I ever hurt you in anyway?"

"No!"

"Well, I'm telling you that if you kill my baby, you will hurt me dearly. Yeah I smoke water, it helps me cope with my mother's death, but it's not going to have no effect on how I treat you and my baby. A family would probably make me more stable."

"I still have to think about school and my future. I don't want to be stuck in the ghetto all of my life, and I don't know what the future holds for us with you being out in them streets doing whatever."

"Robin, you are searching for excuses. If you don't want to have a baby by me just say it, but don't keep coming up with different excuses."

Dirty started putting his clothes back on.

"Where is you going?" she asked him.

"I'm going for a ride. I need to clear my mind." Dirty grabbed his keys off of the dresser and headed out of the house. Robin just laid there curled up with a pillow crying.

Chapter 17

It took Bruce, China Man and Mike about a week to get rid of the jewelry. It wasn't a good lick. The watches that Mike had grabbed were mostly Quartz. there were a couple of Timex watches. But they were not real gold, just gold plated and stainless steel.

Bruce had lost half of the chains when the bag got ripped open. They only got seven thousand combined for the stuff that Bruce and Mike had gotten. They got a little over two thousand apiece. Keith was still in juvenile hall charged with aggravated robbery and felonious assault for the shooting of the old man. The detectives kept going to visit him hoping that he would break, but he remained strong. They threatened to seek getting him bound over as an adult if he did not cooperate. He still wouldn't budge.

Bruce had thought that hitting a jewelry lick would be simple. He did not think that all that had happened would. He now knew that it took more planning to pull off a sophisticated lick. He went up to the plaza to get him a beer. When he came out of the store he seen that there was a dice game going on down in front of the cleaners. He walked down there to see who was all shooting. When he got to the circle he stood up on his toes to see who was inside of the circle shooting. When he seen that it was Vic who had the dice, his blood started to boil. He walked around the circle until he got behind Vic, and then pushed through the circle.

"Hey, watch it!" People said as he pushed through them. Vic had just bent over to roll the dice, when Bruce stole on him hitting him in the side of his face, "Bitch ass nigga! You thought you were going to get away with burning my shit up!" Bruce yelled at him as he drug him out of the circle. Vic never had a chance to recover from the first blow, which had cracked his cheek bone.

Bruce held him by the back of his shirt, collar with his left hand and just kept swinging his right hand hitting Vic in his face. Vic was out on his feet, but Bruce held him up and continued to beat him.

"Bitch ass nigga!"

"Okay, that's enough!" someone from the crowd yelled.

"Fuck that!" Bruce yelled back.

"You done proved your point, what are you trying to do kill him?" The person yelled back at Bruce. Bruce let go of Vic's collar and let him fall to the ground. He went into both of Vic's pockets and pulled out knots of money. He checked his socks and came out with two more knots of money.

Vic was known to keep up to ten thousand dollars on him at all times. Bruce spit on Vic, and then walked off. The crowd was angry at how Bruce did Vic, but no one challenged him, they just did what they could to help Vic once Bruce had left.

Bruce went home and counted up the money he had gotten from Vic. It came up to sixty two hundred. Bruce went back to the same car lot that he had gotten his first car from and bought him another one. That time he got a '77 Buick Regal. Its cost was $6,000.

Bruce bought some knuckle rims for it and some two inch tires and he was down to seven hundred to his name. He decided that he was going to find Dirty to see if he had a lick lined up. He drove up to the Valley in search of Dirty.

Chapter 18

Dirty was up in Rab's parking lot talking to Rab and George. George and Dirty's car were parked side by side. They stood in between the cars talking.

"Damn Dirty, you got two girls pregnant?" George asked him.

"Yeah, that shit is crazy, and it's backwards. That crazy ass hoe Tonya wants to have her baby, but Robin talking about she don't know if she wants to have hers. Man I never knew that bitches could be so much trouble. My mother wasn't like any of these bitches that I been dealing with out here."

"So what are you going to do?" Rab asked him.

"Fuck can I do? I love Robin, that's my boo. If she has an abortion that would take a lot out of me. Fuck all that right now though, we got to make a move to get some money."

"What are you thinking about?" George asked him.

"I'm thinking about hitting another jewelry lick."

"You heard what happened downtown didn't you?"

"No, what happened?"

"Shit! It's been all on the news some niggas hit a jewelry lick downtown and shot the owner of the store. They are still looking for some of the suspects. So it's hot up here as far as that right now." Rab told him.

"Fuck it then, we will take our show on the road."

"What do you mean by that?"

"We are going to go out of town and hit a lick."

"Are you serious?" Rab asked him.

"I'm dead serious, it is going to take a little more planning but we can do it."

A blue Buick Regal pulled up into the parking lot. They watched it approach them. Bruce parked right behind their cars and got out.

"What's up with y'all!" he said to them.

"You change cars like the weather don't you?" Dirty asked him.

"You know how D.T.W. do, ain't no other way like it. I'm trying to get back on the grind. A nigga's pockets done got low. I'm trying to do something."

"We were just talking about doing something. We are going out of town though.

"Why is that?" Bruce asked.

"Some niggas did a lick downtown and shot the owner of the store, so the city is hot right now. We are about to take our show on the road. What's up with your boys, they still want in?"

Bruce knew that Dirty was referring to the lick that they had hit. He figured if Dirty found out that he was the reason that the city was hot, that he wouldn't let him be down on the lick, so he kept quiet on that.

"Yeah they want to get down."

"We are going to all get together this weekend to go over shit, and then we are on the road."

"Are we driving our own shit?" Bruce asked him.

"I'm going to drive my car down there, but we are going to steal one from down there to hit the lick in. So I hope one of your dudes know how to steal cars, cause we are going to need someone who can do that."

"Don't worry! I got that covered."

"Have your boys up at the courts Friday at five. We are going to pull down there so we can chop it up and figure everything out."

"That's a bet!" Bruce said, then got back in his car and pulled off. He knew that Mike was the go to guy for stealing the cars, so his end was straight. It would be him China Man and Mike. He headed back down the way to put them up on game.

Chapter 19

Robin was sitting up in her biology class, when all of a sudden she felt wetness in between her legs. She looked down and seen that the front of her pants had a dark red stain in her crotch area. She jumped out of her chair and headed for the door, "Jacobs where do you think you're going?" asked the teacher, as Robin snatched opens the classroom door.

"My baby! My baby!" Robin sobbed. Lynn jumped up out of her chair and ran after Robin. Robin ran to the infirmary and told them that she needed help. Instead of giving her immediate attention, one of the nurses told her to take a seat on the bench. Lynn stepped forward and yelled at the nurse, "She needs help now dammit! She is pregnant and bleeding!" The nurse was startled at Lynn's aggression. She got up and came around the counter and seen that the front of Robin's pants was covered in blood.

"Okay, help me get her onto the examination table!" The nurse said to Lynn. Together they helped Robin up onto the table, "Take this pager and go page Dirty at 663-2038. When he pages you back call that number and tell him what is going on!"

"663-2038 okay!" Lynn said as she rushed out of the room. She went down the hall by the principal's office, where there were two payphones and she paged Dirty.

The nurse had called for the paramedics to come and take Robin to the hospital. By the time that they got there, blood was all over the table. Dirty had still not called back.

The paramedics loaded Robin into the ambulance. They allowed Lynn to ride with them to the hospital. On the ride to the hospital Robin's pager started beeping. There was no way for Lynn to return the call.

Once they got to the hospital, they rushed Robin into the emergency room and Lynn headed for the payphones. She dialed the number that the page had come from and was surprised when she heard George's voice answer the phone, "George, where is Dirty at?"

"Who is this?"

"It's Lynn"

"So, you ain't got no holla for me?"

"Now ain't the time George, something has happened to Robin and I need to speak to Dirty."

"Alright, but I'm trying to see you, you hear me?"

"Yeah, I hear you." George passed Dirty the phone.

"Hello?"

"Dirty we are up at Kaiser hospital. Something is wrong with Robin and the baby. You need to come up here!"

"I'm on my way!" Dirty told her then hung up.

"What's wrong with Robin?" Rab asked him.

"I don't know, but I'm about to go and find out!" Dirty told him as he headed out the door.

Dirty stormed up to Kaiser hospital. By the time he got there, Robin had been placed in her room. Lynn was standing in the hallway when he approached, "She lost it Dirty!" she told him. Dirty went to the doorway of Robin's room and looked in at her. She was sitting up in bed crying. Her eyes were almost swollen shut.

She looked up and seen Dirty standing in the doorway. "I'm sorry, I'm so sorry. Dirty did not go to her to give her any comfort. He did not say one word to her. He just turned and left, "Dirty where are you going!" Lynn asked him when he walked passed her. Dirty did not answer her, he just kept walking out of the hospital. He jumped into his car and headed down to King Kennedy. He did not know how to feel. He wondered had Robin purposefully did something to cause herself to miscarry, being as she acted as if she did not want the baby anyway.

He pulled up on Bundy drive and bought him a dipped cigarette for twenty five dollars, then headed to Tonya's house.

When he got there, Tonya opened the door and was happy to see him. She threw her arms around him and tried to kiss him in the mouth. Dirty pushed her off of him and walked into her house. He went into her bedroom, sat on her bed, pulled his shoes off and lit up the cigarette. The smell of the PCP hit Tonya and caused her to start to fiend. She sat on the bed next to Dirty and watched him smoke. She tried to inhale the smoke that Dirty was blowing out of his mouth, "Let me hit that Dirty."

"Aren't you pregnant?"

"One little hit ain't go hurt nothing." Dirty passed her the cigarette and she took more than one little hit.

Tonya took three deep long pulls. She let them out, and then took two more pulls. Dirty snatched the cigarette out of her hand.

"You're crazy ass don't need that much of that shit!" he told her. He leaned back on the headboard and smoked. Tonya hadn't smoked water since the night that she had pulled the knife on Dirty. Those deep pulls had taken an instant effect on her. As always she started feeling hot, which caused her to strip naked? She got on the bed and undid Dirty's pants. She reached inside of his boxers and pulled out his dick and balls.

She started sucking on his balls. The sensation that Dirty got from her sucking on his balls spread throughout his body. His toes even started to tingle. Tonya took his dick into her mouth and deep throated him. Dirty started to choke on the smoke. He had to put the cigarette down.

Wet turned Tonya into a sexual beast. She rose up and pulled Dirty's pants and drawers off of him, then she jumped on top of him and started riding him reversed cow girl style. She put her hands on his thighs and jumped up and down on his dick. She was in a zone and started talking crazy to Dirty.

"That bitch can't fuck you like me. Nigga I work this pussy. You need a woman nigga, not a child. Watch me work this pussy." She sat all the way down on him and started rotating her hips. Her pussy was super wet and leaking fluids. The hair on Dirty's dick was soaking wet. He felt stickiness all the way up to his navel.

"Watch momma pull that nut from you!" She told him as she started rotating her hips in the other direction. She grinded on him. Dirty was high as hell, but that did not stop him from busting a powerful nut inside of her, before he fell out snoring. Tonya looked down at him and said, "I put that ass to sleep!" Then she fell on top of him and passed out.

Chapter 20

Robin had been at Dirty's house for the past three days and he had not come home period. She had continuously paged him over those past three days and he never returned any of her calls. She had started to become worried about him. She even called his grandmother Ms. Pearl, who said that she had not seen or heard from him. Robin figured that she would have Lynn holla at George to see if she could find out anything.

Ÿ

Dirty had been staying at Tonya's house for the past three days. He had been in a depressed mood that was hard for him to come out of. He had been getting Robin's pages, but just didn't feel like talking to her. It hurt him to know that she couldn't accept him the way he was. Who was she to tell him that he needed help?

Tonya accepted him the way he was. She didn't care that he smoked water. Plus she sucked and fucked him into a feeling of bliss. He had even started to look forward to her having his baby.

It was Friday and he knew that he had to shake that feeling of depression. He had moves to make. He had Tonya wash, dry and iron his clothes, while he took a bath. After he got out of the tub, he called George and told him to meet him at Rab's house.

Tonya talked Dirty into eating some breakfast while she waited on his clothes to dry. Dirty sat down at the kitchen table wearing nothing but a towel and ate an egg omelet, some bacon and toast. Tonya dropped down to her knees, climbed under the table and started sucking Dirty's dick. She sucked him until he came in her mouth. She sucked him dry and licked him clean. She thought that the way that she was sexing Dirty would keep him coming back. She went and got his clothes out of the dryer and ironed them. When she got finished, Dirty got dressed and bounced.

He headed up to Rab's house. When he got up there Rab and George were standing in the parking lot. They climbed into his car and he headed down the way. He pulled up to the basketball court and Bruce was there with two of his boys.

Rab and George got out of the car and approached Bruce and his boys. They all shook hands and formed a circle, "So what's the plan?" Bruce asked Dirty.

"First off, you are going to have to drive your own car, same as me. Six people can't fit in my two door car. But the plan is we are going to drive out to Elyria and hit Service Merchandise in the Midway mall. My boy Darrin been staying out there since he got placed in a group home out there. He said it's sweet. We are going to check it out and if it is sweet we are going to hit it. Do y'all have hammers?"

"Why everybody keep talking about hammers, all we need is these." Mike said pulling the bearings out of his pocket. Dirty looked at the bearing and remembered the day that he saw Ron bust a forty ounce bottle with one.

"Them things work good?" Dirty asked him.

"They are the truth, ask Bruce, he seen them work." Bruce thought back to them hitting the jewelry store then said, "They are official, we don't need no hammers!"

"Okay then, let's go." everybody looked at Dirty.

"Go where?" Bruce asked him.

"We are going out to Elyria. We got to case the spot, and peep out the getaway route."

"How far is Elyria from here?"

"About thirty miles,"

"I got to put gas in my tank then." Bruce told him.

"Okay, I'm going to follow you to the gas station."

Bruce and his crew jumped in his car and Dirty and his crew got back in his. Dirty followed Bruce to a Shell gas station on 40th and Quincy and they both filled up their gas tanks, and then Dirty took the lead. He drove down to 30th and Woodland then jumped onto the freeway. He took 90 east and then drove for about thirty minutes, then got off the freeway at the exit that said welcome to Elyria.

They drove around a circular ramp that took them to a straight away. At the second light on their left side was the Midway mall.

Dirty pulled into the mall with Bruce following him. It was a big mall and the parking lot was full of cars. It was 7:30 in the evening and the mall was still open. They made two trips around the mall looking for a Service Merchandise, but couldn't find it.

Dirty decided to circle the lot one more time. When he got to the back of the mall he looked across the street and seen that it was another shopping center across the street.

He pulled out of the mall and pulled over into the shopping center. There it was next to a Value City store. "Service Merchandise, there it is," Dirty said smiling. He pulled into a parking space and Bruce pulled in next to him. Dirty exited his car, "I will be back." he told George and Rab. He called for Bruce to join him. Bruce got out of his car, "What's up playboy?"

"Me and you are going in to case the spot. It only takes two of us. We don't want to look suspicious." They went into the store, which was gigantic. The store sold more than just jewelry.

They located the jewelry section, which was huge and had lots of display cases. Dirty and Bruce roamed from case to case, seeing which ones had the best jewelry. After they selected three cases, they walked around the store seeing what type of security it had. To their surprise, they could not find one security guard and there was a clear shot to the door from the jewelry section.

They left out of the store and went back to their cars. Bruce followed Dirty as he pulled out of the shopping center, drove down the street and pulled into a McDonald's parking lot. He pulled into the drive thru and placed orders and Bruce did the same. After they got their food they pulled into the back of the restaurant and parked. They got out of the cars leaned on the cars, and ate their food as Dirty told them the plan.

"Look, it's going down tomorrow morning. Who is stealing the car Bruce?"

"That will be me." Mike answered.

"We are going to pick up my boy Darrin and he is going to take us around to find a car. We are looking for a big car, like a station wagon. We get it tonight and park it until the morning. We are going to park our cars in the mall's parking lot, and use the hottie to drive over there to hit the lick. Now, it's six of us and we need three drivers, one for Bruce car, one for mine and one for the hottie. Me and Bruce are going in. Who wants to be the third one?"

"Me! No doubt!" George said.

"Anybody got a problem with that?" Dirty asked them and nobody said anything.

"Okay, there it is, Rab you drive my car." Mike broke in, "Since I got to steal the hottie, I might as well drive it."

"That leaves you China man, to drive Bruce's car. I got to go to the payphone to call my boy right quick." Dirty walked to the front of McDonald's and found a payphone. He called Darrin and got directions, then went back and had everybody get into the cars. He followed the directions that Darrin gave him and they led him to the Wilks Villa housing projects. He pulled into a back parking lot and Darrin was standing outside waiting on him.

Dirty got out of the car and him and Darrin approached each other and gave each other a hug. Darrin use to run heavy with Dirty up in Cleveland until he got in trouble. The judge sent him to a group home out in Elyria. From there he was placed in foster care. Darrin's brother William went out there to visit him one day and met this girl named Lilly.

William ended up moving out there with Lilly and they got custody of Darrin.

"What's up?" Darrin asked Dirty.

"We came out here to hit that lick. I need you to take us to a good place to steal a car."

"Okay, come on." They walked over to Dirty's car, and Dirty told George to get into the back seat. George climbed out of the front and got into the back and Darrin climbed into the front seat.

Darrin directed them to a city that was smaller than Elyria called Oberlin. They pulled into an apartment complex, where they had seen a Buick station wagon.

Mike got out of Bruce's car and approached the station wagon. He grabbed the driver's side door handle and was surprise that the door was unlocked. He quickly jumped in the car, peeled the column and started the car up. He followed them back to Darrin's place. They parked the car, then Darrin took them on a tour of the city that ended at a girl named Shelly's house. Shelly's mother was hardly ever home and their house was like the neighborhood flop house.

Shelly was happy to have some boys from out of town stay the night over her house. She showed them all hospitality, by fucking each one of them. She even woke some of them up during the night to offer them seconds.

Ÿ

At nine the next morning Dirty got up and started waking everybody else up. They all got in the cars, took Darrin home and picked up the hottie.

They rode back out to Midway mall, and found parking spots next to each other. They got out of the cars again to go over the plan one more time. "Give us some of them pellets," Dirty told mike. Mike reached in his pocket and came out with a handful of bearings. He handed them to Dirty and he split them up between him, George and Bruce.

"Alright y'all! It's time to go. Look we already scoped out the cases. George I'm going to point to the case that I want you to hit and I want you to go right at it, no hesitation. Soon as me and Bruce get to our cases we are hitting them. Y'all got it?" They both shook their heads yeah. He turned to China Man and Rab,   "Y'all sit in the cars and keep them running."

They got into the station wagon and Mike pulled off. He pulled out of the Mall's parking lot, and pulled over into the shopping center's parking lot.

"Pull right up to the door. We want them to see this car, that way it's the car that they will be looking for. Here take these bags for the jewelry," Dirty told them.

Mike pulled to a stop right in front of the sliding doors, and they got out of the car. Dirty led the way headed straight for the jewelry section.

"Hit that one George," Dirty told him pointing to a case. George headed for the case, and Dirty and Bruce went separate ways. Each of them already had pellets in their hands as they approached the cases.

George was the first one to throw his bearing, which shattered the glass in the display case. Dirty, then Bruce hit their cases and started snatching jewelry. The way the bearings smashed the cases gave workers and customers the impression that someone was shooting. They started running and ducking for cover. By the time they realized what was really going on, Dirty and his crew were headed out of the door.

They jumped into the station wagon, "Go! Go!" Dirty yelled to Mike who threw the car in drive and burned rubber pulling off. Workers ran to the door and seen the car flying out of the lot. Mike shot across the street into the mall's parking lot. He pulled up to their cars, and Dirty instantly got heated, China Man was sitting on the hood of Bruce's car talking to two young white girls. The girls were startled when the station wagon drove up fast, stopped and out jumped four black guys. They just stood there and looked as the boys started jumping into Dirty and Bruce's car.

"Let's go nigga!" Dirty yelled at China Man who was still intent on getting the girls number. Rab pulled out of the lot calmly and headed to the freeway with China Man following him. "Fuck is wrong with that dumb ass nigga. Them bitches seen my car, and they seen our faces, this shit is crazy!" Dirty said just ranting.

Rab jumped back onto the freeway, "Make sure that you do the limit," Dirty told Rab.

Rab looked and seen that he was doing sixty seven and let his foot up off of the gas a little bit.

They made it back to Cleveland. "Go up to your house," Dirty told Rab. They went up to Rab's house and before the car fully stopped Dirty jumped out and ran over to Bruce's car and began yelling through the window at China Man.

"You dumb ass nigga! Fuck is wrong with you! You ain't getting shit!" Everybody jumped out of the cars. China Man wasn't use to nobody talking to him like that and he quickly got upset.

"Fuck you nigga! I'll beat your bitch ass nigga, I better get my money!" China Man said advancing on Dirty. Everybody got between them to keep them apart.

"Chill Dirty we are in the clear!" Bruce told him.

"Nigga!"

"Them bitches had seen our faces and our cars."

"I got to get rid of this car."

"That's your boy Bruce, but don't ever bring him around me no more."

"He can't ever do shit with me, not even just kick it."

"Let's go into the house and split this shit up!"

Dirty thought that it was better to just split up the merchandise and let Bruce and his boys get gone. So they went into Rab's house and laid out all the jewelry. They organized it by the price range and each took turns picking a piece until all the jewelry was gone. After they split up the jewelry, Bruce and his crew went their separate way.

Dirty, Rab and George then put to the side jewelry that they wanted to keep for themselves. They each kept a ring, a chain and a watch. After that, Dirty and Rab jumped in George's car.

"George pulls down on 75th so I can see if that nigga Donny is down there. George drove down the hill to the weed strip. Donny was down there sitting on his motorcycle. Dirty got out of the car and approached him, "Donny I need you."

"Shit! you ought to make me part of your click, as much as you be needing me!" Donny said with a smile.

"Seriously, Donny I need you to burn my car up."

"Burn it up? What you doing an insurance job?"

"No, I hit a lick and somebody seen my car. I can't take a chance. I have to report it stolen. You can have everything, the rims, tires and the system. Just take it somewhere and burn it."

"Where is it at?"

"Up in Rab's parking lot. Do you need the keys?"

"Fuck I need the keys for? I got you!" Donny cranked up his motorcycle and headed up the hill and Dirty got back into George's car.

"Go up to Hobo's store." George drove up to Hobo's and Dirty got out and went into the store. Hobo was behind the counter, "What's up Hobo?" Hobo looked up, "Dirty my man, where you been?"

"I been on the grind, look I need you to call Lou. I got this jewelry that I want him to see."

"Okay, I will do that for you. Dirty I just want you to know that whatever business that you and Lou be involved in, that I have nothing to do with it. I do not want you feeling some type of way towards me behind what y'all go through. Matter of fact my mother knows a lot of fences that deals in jewelry, and she might can off the stuff for you. If you want me to, I will call her."

"Yeah, do that." Hobo called his mother Mary and she was there within twenty minutes. Mary entered the store, and Dirty was surprised at how young she looked. She also was dressed fly like a young girl. She had a guy with her that looked to be about Hobo's age. Dirty thought that he was probably Hobo's brother, but later found out that it was Mary's boyfriend.

Hobo introduced them, "Ma, this is Dirty Red. He is a natural hustler, and he has some jewelry that he would like for you to see."

"What do you got for me baby?" Mary asked Dirty while looking him up and down as if she wanted to eat him.

"Let me go get my boys right quick." Dirty left out of the store and reentered with George and Rab. Hobo let them go into the office in back of the store. They each took turns dumping their jewelry out onto the desk so that Mary could appraise it. She was amazed at the type and quality of the jewelry.

They had fifteen thousand dollar Rolex watches, ten thousand dollar Cartier watches. They had five thousand dollar diamond tennis bracelets and ten thousand dollar diamond engagement rings.

All together they had over $350,000 worth of jewelry.

Mary told them, "I can probably get y'all a third of that, which is $116,666, and I'm going to have to get a $2,500 commission."

"Are you serious?" Dirty asked her.

"Listen baby, ain't nothing in life free. Do you think realtors and stock brokers do what they do for free? You spend money to make money. You boys are young and greedy right now. If you last in this game you will learn how things really go. Now do we have a deal or what?"

Dirty looked to George, then to Rab and then to her, "Yeah we got a deal."

"Okay, let me make a couple of calls right quick. I'm going to need y'all to step outside of the office for a minute." Dirty and his crew stepped out of the office, and Mary made some calls. She came out of the office and said, "Okay baby you are going to have to follow me. When we get there, you are going to be the only one that can come in with me. My buyer does not like meeting many people. Let's go, he is waiting for us." They all went outside. Mary and her boyfriend got into their van. Dirty and his crew got in George's car, and George followed the van.

They traveled out to Chagrin Falls, where the rich white people lived. They turned onto a side street that had houses that looked like baby mansions, with long driveways. The van turned into one of those driveways and pulled up to a three story brick house.

Mary got out of the van and signaled for Dirty to join her. Dirty got out of the car and followed Mary to the side door of the house. Mary rang the doorbell and after a few seconds, a middle aged Hispanic woman wearing a maid's uniform opened the door.

"Mr. Greztski is awaiting you." the maid told them as she let them in. She led them through the kitchen and down the hall to a room that had been converted into an office.

The maid led them into the office, where an older white man sat behind a big mahogany desk. Dirty looked at the man and knew that he wasn't American. The man looked of Russian descent. When he spoke he had a very deep accent, "Mary my love, you have brought me something good?"

"Yes Marty, I have some magnificent pieces for you." She turned to Dirty, "Could you pass me the bags please?" and Dirty handed her the bags of jewelry.

Mary dumped each bag out onto the desk. He reached inside of the top drawer of the desk and removed a pair of glasses and put them on. He started to examine each piece of jewelry, "Very nice!" he said while examining the jewelry.

He looked at Mary, "And you say that the total price is what?"

"$350,000 and a third of that is $116,666 thousand."

"This young man that you have with you, does these items belong to him?"

"Yes they do!" Marty turned to Dirty, "What is your name?"

"Dirty Red," Marty laughed, "Dirty Red, how did you get a name like that?"

"My mother gave it to me," Dirty told him as he started to get angry.

"Do you have a real name?"

"Yeah, it's Tyrone."

"I like Tyrone much better. Well Tyrone, I like how you think, you think big. A lot of people think small, but you think big. Me and you may possibly do much business together. You do good by me and I will do good by you. Do we understand each other?"

"Yeah, I understand you!"

"Good, and since you are ambitious, I am going to give you what you are expecting. Usually I would try to negotiate for a better price and get you to come down, way down, but I like you.

Mary the two of you wait right here, I will be right back. Marty left the office and went to his bedroom. He went to his wall safe and removed $116,700 then headed back to the office. He sat down at his desk then pushed the money across the desk, "There you go $116,700."

"That's over," Dirty told him.

"Don't worry about it, just look at it as a tip." Marty told Dirty smiling.

Dirty grabbed the money counted out twenty five hundred and handed it to Mary. He told Marty thanks and turned to leave.

"Hey Tyrone!" Dirty turned back around and Marty said to him, "When you play in the big leagues, you meet big and powerful people. People that can be a asset to you again someday," He turned to Mary, "Thank you, and please keep in touch." Mary and Dirty headed out of the house. Before they got outside, Mary passed Dirty a card with her number on it.

"I like you Dirty, me and you could do some things together, a lot of things." she told him then licked her lips seductively. They exited the house, got back in the vehicles and George followed the van until they got back to the city limits, then they went their separate ways.

"Go to my house?" Dirty told George.

George drove to Dirty's house and they all got out of the car. Dirty opened the door and they entered. They knew that there were people in the house from the voices that they heard coming from the living room. They all went to the living room. Robin and Lynn were sitting on the couch with their legs folded underneath them.

Robin looked up at Dirty with a look that could kill. Dirty turned around, "Come on y'all." he said to George and Rab. He led them upstairs to his bedroom. Dirty flopped down on the bed, pulled the money out and started splitting it up into three piles. When he got finished there was a little over thirty eight thousand in each pile. He grabbed his and told George and Rab to grab theirs. Dirty turned to walk over to the dresser and noticed Robin standing in the doorway with her arms folded across her chest.

"What's up?" Dirty asked her.

"You are just going to come up in here and ignore me. I haven't seen your ass in almost a week."

"Don't you see that I'm doing something?"

"Fuck that! George, Rab could y'all please go downstairs so I can talk to him?" Rab and George left out of the room closing the door behind them. Robin started back up, "You have been avoiding me and I want to know why? I lost my baby and been dealing with the shit by myself, while your ass has been out running the streets doing who knows what!"

"Robin, I ain't trying to hear that shit."

"You ain't want the baby anyway."

"You probably caused yourself to miscarry."

"Is you fucking crazy! Is that what you think, that I killed our baby. Yeah I had doubts at first, but I had already made up my mind that I was going to have the baby. I wouldn't have done anything without talking to you first. Don't you get it! I love you! You are my first and only love. I have been going crazy wondering about you. I even had thoughts of suicide that is why Lynn is over here. She had to talk some sense into me."

Dirty tucked his money under the shirts in his drawer, closed it and walked out of the room. Robin followed him to the stairs. She stood at the top while he went down them, "You ain't go just dog me Dirty. You can run all you want, but I will still be here when you get back!"

Dirty got downstairs and seen that George was sitting on the couch with his arm draped around Lynn and was all in her ear. Lynn was just sitting there grinning from ear to ear.

"Let's go y'all!" Dirty told Rab and George.

"So, what's up?" George asked Lynn.

"I got to go home and get a change of clothes."

"You do that, and I will see you when we get back." George told her as he headed out of the door. When they got outside Dirty asked George, "What was all that about?"

"I told her to stay at your house tonight and that I will take her shopping tomorrow."

"So, you're tricking now?"

"If tricking equals me dicking, then so be it." George said laughing.

They all got into the car, "Rab is you going to the house or what? I'm 'bout to have George shoot me up to my uncle's house, then down to K.K, and then I'm headed in."

"You about to get some water?" Rab asked him.

"Yeah, I got to get high to deal with Robin's ass."

"I want to get me a stick too, before I go in."

"Okay George shoot down to King Kennedy first."

George drove down to Bundy drive, and Dirty copped a dipped cigarette and a joint from Tex. He got in the car and passed Rab the joint. He stuck the cigarette that was wrapped inside of aluminum foil into his pocket.

George drove up to the Valley. They dropped Rab off then drove around the bend and pulled into Loft's parking lot. Dirty got out and went to Loft's apartment. He knocked and loft answered the door.

"Man, where you been?"

"Hittin' licks unc."

"You good?"

"I need you to get me another car."

"Where the Park Avenue at?"

"Somebody stole it."

"Somebody stole it and you are going to just go out and buy another one?"

"Yep, and don't worry, I'm going to shoot you a couple thousand dollars. I appreciate everything that you have done for me."

"Nigga it ain't about no money with me. You're my little sister's boy. I do what I do out of love. I just wish you would change up. You keep getting money, but ain't doing nothing with it. You see how I flipped them four ounces for you. That's where the easy money is at. You could sale work."

"That ain't me unc. You like doing what you do, and I like doing what I do. I'm still going to throw you the two grand on G.P. Me and George are going to come and pick you up Monday morning, to go to the car lot."

"Yeah okay nephew, Red do me a favor be careful and go see your grandmother she has been asking about you."

"I got you unc." Dirty told him then headed out the house.

He jumped back into the car with George and they headed back to Dirty's house. When they got there Lynn and Robin were sitting on the couch wearing night gowns. Dirty and George sat down with them. Dirty pulled the cigarette out of his pocket and lit it. He took two deep pulls paused then took two more. He told Robin to pass the cigarette to George, who was sitting on the other side of her.

Robin took the cigarette, but instead of passing it to George she started smoking it. The combination of the weed and PCP was too much for her lungs and she went into a fit of coughing. She reached her arm out to hand the cigarette to George, who took it. George only puffed on it lightly. Lynn looked on in amusement. After seeing Robin hit it, she wanted to hit it, "Pass it to me George." He passed it to her and she inhaled and exhaled three times. She got up and walked, over to Dirty and handed the cigarette to him. The cigarette went around two more times, before it was gone.

Robin, who was zooted grabbed Dirty's hand, "Come on, let's go to bed." She pulled Dirty up off of the couch and led him upstairs. They went into the bedroom and Robin closed the door. She stripped naked and helped Dirty get naked. She then dropped down onto her knees and started giving Dirty head. Dirty just stood there with his hands on his hips looking down watching Robin's head bob up and down on his dick.

Robin was being aggressive. The wet had her going. She was slurping and slobbering all on his dick. She stood up went over to the dresser and grabbed a jar of Vaseline. She went back over to Dirty, handed him the jar and told him, "Put some of that on your dick." She climbed onto the bed and got on her hands and knees, facing the mirror that sat on the dresser.

Dirty lube his dick up with the Vaseline. He figured that her pussy must have been dry. Robin reached both of her arms back and used her hands to spread her ass cheeks. Dirty walked up behind her, took his hand and positioned his dick to her pussy's entrance.

"Not there, put it in my ass!" Robin told him, then reached behind her and lifted Dirty's dick up to the entrance of her asshole. Dirty put his hands on her hips and pushed forward. The head of his dick stretched her asshole open, "Go slow Dirty."

Dirty slowly pushed his dick all the way into Robin's ass until all that remained outside was his balls. He started fucking her slowly. They both locked eyes in the mirror, like they were looking into each other's soul.

Tears formed at the corners of Robin's eyes. She hopes that what she was doing proved to Dirty how much she loved him. Dirty had never in his life felt such a feeling as he was getting from fucking Robin in her ass. The sensation started to become overwhelming. He started letting his animalistic instincts come out. He growled as he started fucking Robin's asshole with brute force.

Robin's asshole muscles had already adjusted to Dirty's dick. She had started to feel more pleasure than pain. She put her elbows down on the bed, leaned down on them, and then started rocking back and forth on her knees. She started matching Dirty thrust for thrust.

Dirty's whole body started to tremble. He realized that he was breathing heavily. He looked back into the mirror and seen that he was completely covered in sweat. He took the back of his hand to wipe the sweat from his forehead. He felt as if his body was rapidly heating up. Still he pounded Robin's asshole ferociously. His balls started to tingle and his nut shot up through his dick. As he was busting off in Robin, he became light headed and his legs gave out and Dirty crashed to the floor.

Robin looked back and jumped up, "Dirty! Dirty!" she pulled on his arm, but he wouldn't respond, "Shit!" Robin said as she grabbed her gown and put it on. She ran out of the room yelling.

"Lynn, George help!" she got no answer. She ran down the steps and into the living room and seen that George had Lynn on the floor with her knees damn near touching her head as he fucked her. She heard George telling her "I told you that you would come in, they all do."

"George! Lynn! Y'all help me, Dirty passed out and I can't get him up." George jumped up and pulled his pants back on, "Get some ice, some milk and a spoon!" George told Robin as he ran up the stairs.

Robin ran into the kitchen and grabbed a tray of ice out of the freezer, a quart of milk out of the refrigerator and a spoon out of the dish rack. She ran up the stairs.

Lynn was standing outside of the door out of respect for Dirty being naked. Robin went into the room, handed George the milk and spoon and cracked the ice in the ice tray. Robin put ice in both of her hands and started rubbing it all over Dirty's head and face. George stuck the spoon into Dirty's mouth and forced it open then started pouring milk into his mouth. Dirty coughed and opened his eyes.

"Keep the ice on him!" George told Robin as he forced Dirty up into a sitting position so that he wouldn't choke on the milk. He tilted Dirty's head back and continued to pour milk down his throat. After a couple of minutes, Dirty was able to get up off of the floor and sit on the bed.

"Do he need to go to the hospital?" Robin asked George.

"No he was just dehydrated and his body overheated. He's going to be alright, just make him keep drinking that milk. I got some unfinished business to tend to. Come on Lynn, let me finish tapping that ass." he said to her, and then slapped her on the ass. Lynn just smiled and followed him back downstairs.

Robin could not believe how Lynn was getting down, little Ms. stuck up. She thought to herself, that it had to be the water that got her open like that. She forced Dirty to finish the rest of the quart of milk. He got up, went into the bathroom, washed his face and took a piss. When he went back into the bedroom he felt better. They both got into the bed and went to sleep in each other's arms.

Ÿ

Bruce and his crew were at the courts playing basketball. They were showing out, playing basketball in all their jewelry. They had on several gold chains, gold rings and gold watches. Bruce even had on a half carat earring.

He had his new car, an Audi parked on the sidewalk in front of the court. The Regal was up there too, only it belonged to China man then, who had it painted candy apple red, and had a red rag top put on it.

Mike's car was up there too. He had purchased a Mustang 5.0 with a drop top. Bruce, China Man and Mike were on the same team. They were showing out letting their chains swing loosely around their necks as they ran up and down the court, "Y'all niggas can't fuck with us!" Bruce hollered at the other team after dunking in their face.

Everybody down the way had started to envy Bruce and his crew. They were draped in jewelry and had fly rides. People gave them their props. A lot of niggas tried to get down with them but they played them off.

They did not make as much money off of their jewelry as Dirty and his crew did. They didn't have any connects and had to sale their jewelry on the streets, often at ridiculous prices. They ended up keeping a lot of jewelry for themselves also.

After Bruce bought his car, he had about seven thousand dollars left. But that was quickly diminishing as he continued to splurge on anything that he could. Also he went from just drinking beer to smoking wet on the regular.

He was enjoying his self as if he did not have a care in the world. No one paid attention to the blue Skylark that pulled up, or the little short bald headed guy that got out of the car and approached the court. It wasn't until he reached the sideline and people started to notice that he had a gun in his hand, and then all hell started to break loose. People started running and yelling, "He got a gun! He got a gun!" The players stopped to see what was going on.

When Bruce looked up Vic was standing right in front of him. "So we meet again youngster!" Vic said as he raised the gun. Bruce turned and took off running. Vic took a steady aim and let off four shots, three of which hit Bruce.

He hit Bruce twice in his shoulder and once in his leg. Bruce fell to the ground and laid still. Vic turned around and walked calmly back to the Skylark, got in and pulled off.

China Man, Mike and a couple others ran ever to help Bruce. When they reached him, he was lying on his stomach. China Man turned him over onto his back. Bruce opened his eyes and asked, "Is he gone?"

"Yeah he gone!" China Man told him.

"Alright help me up." Bruce said as he sat up. They all had thought that Bruce was dead or seriously injured. But Bruce had played possum. They helped him up to his feet and he put his good arm around China Man.

"I'm going to kill that bitch ass nigga!" Bruce said as he hopped to the car.

They took him to Charity hospital where he was treated for three flesh wounds. Miraculously all the bullets had went straight through without hitting any vital organs. Bruce received stitches and bandages and was released.

Ÿ

Ron and Tim both went to court together and were assigned public defenders. They both found out that there was only one statement against them. The one that the old lady had wrote. Their attorneys told them that they had some good news and some bad news for them. The good news was that the murder charge had been dropped down to manslaughter, because the elements of the crime did not fit the description of a murder charge. Also the lawyers told them that there was no evidence to prove robbery or attempted robbery. The bad news, the lawyers informed them was that the prosecutor was seeking to have them both bound over and tried as adults. They advised them that manslaughter in the adult system carried five to twenty five years. They assured them that they were going to do all that they could do to try to keep them from being bound over, starting with a psychological evaluation.

Ron asked his attorney, "Is there any way that I can take out, and they let my partner go?"

"It's not you that's hurting him, it's the witness statement, that she witnessed you two do those acts many of times together."

"Yeah, but she ain't see him do anything. She really didn't see me do anything. Talk to the prosecutor. Tell him I will take total responsibility if he lets Timothy go."

"Okay I will talk to him and see what he says."

On the ride back to the detention home Ron told Tim, "I talked to my lawyer, and told him to tell the prosecutor that I will take out if he lets you go."

"Man, you don't have to do that?"

"That's what real niggas do dawg. Ain't no sense in us both going down. Somebody needs to be on the street to look out for the other."

"You know what's crazy?"

"What?"

"We ain't heard shit from that nigga Mike."

"I know I heard he out there driving a car now and everything."

"We got to get up with that nigga. He can't leave his boys hanging." Ron said.

"I got his number."

"When we get back give it to me and I'm going to have the counselor give me a call."

"Okay bet."

Chapter 21

Dirty was riding around in his new car. Loft had taken him back to Rick's trading post, where he purchased a 1984 Camaro. It was all black with T-tops. Dirty had an Alpine stereo system put in it, and had the car fitted with some all chrome alloy rims.

George had given his mother the Regency and had bought him a 1983 Cadillac Fleetwood. George was fly to death. He was still going to school, driving his car and draped in jewelry. He had locked Lynn in she was officially his girl. She stayed with him twenty four seven, the same way that Robin stayed with Dirty.

Rab moved his mother out of the projects. He put down seventy five hundred towards buying a house. He put the house in his mother's name, and set up a bank account for her to help her pay the mortgage of six hundred and fifty dollars. They had gotten a house up near the 93rd and Union area. It was a single family, four bedroom home. Rab had the basement of the house fixed up and turned into a recreation room. There were pool tables, arcade games and racing tracks.

For some reason Rab did not buy a car. He bought himself a little scooter. He would ride around on his scooter wearing the flyest gear and draped in jewelry. Rab was really thinking ahead of Dirty and George. He was investing his money in things such as the house. He spent five thousand dollars and bought eight pounds of weed. He started fronting the younger boys the weed to sell for him on the block, and he would just ride around on his scooter all day continuously stopping on the block to pick up money and drop off more weed.

Dirty asked him one day, "What you a dope boy now?"

"I'm a money getter Dirty, and anyway that I can get money, I'm going to get it. This don't mean that I ain't down with hittin' licks no more."

"Whenever you call me I'm going to be ready. I just want to get money as many ways as I can."

"I don't never want me and my family to live the way that we used to before I hooked up with you!"

"Hobo tried to put me on before maybe I will holla at him. We got to hit one more lick though. I'm thinking about going to Pennsylvania on a Greyhound. I'm still mapping it out, but when I get all of the information it's on."

Chapter 22

Ron's counselor allowed him to have a phone call and he called Mike. Mike's mother answered the phone, "Hello?"

"Ms. Hamilton, is Mike there?"

"Who is this?"

"It's Ronald."

"Oh hey Ronald, I heard that you are locked up, are you okay in there?"

"Yes ma'am."

"Okay, hold on."

She yelled out to Mike, "Mike come and get this phone!" Mike picked the phone up, "What's up nigga?"

"Who this Ron?"

"Yeah, it's Ron nigga!"

"What's up dawg?"

"Oh, so I'm your dawg, but neither me nor Tim have heard from your ass. That's fucked up we hear that you're doing your thing out there and we are in here about to get sent up forever."

"It ain't like that dawg, you niggas just haven't gotten with me to let me know what y'all need."

"We need lawyers. They are trying to bound us over as adults and give us five to twenty five years. I'm trying to take out and free Tim, but my public defender says he doubts that they will go for it. You know what they say, a public defender is just a public pretender. You get us a lawyer and shit might work out a little better for us."

"So give me a lawyer's name and number."

"Get a pen and paper."

"Okay, hold up." Mike went and got a pen and a piece of paper off his dresser and went back to the phone, "Okay give it to me."

"His name is Tom Mancino and his number is 255-0326. Dude that gave me his number says that he is good and cheap. He got dude two years in ODYS for four robberies."

"I will call him first thing in the morning, that's my word."

"Alright man, I'm going to hold you to it too. I'm going to tell Tim that you say you got us."

"When can you call back?"

"I don't know, why?"

"If you can call back tomorrow about this time, I can tell you what's up."

"Okay, I'm going to do that. I will get up with you." Ron told him, then hung up.

Ÿ

Keith was bound over and charged as an adult. He was charged with aggravated robbery and felonious assault. He went before a judge and was given a $50,000 bond. He had his mother call China Man on the three way conference call. China Man picked up the phone, "Hello?"

"I need y'all man!"

"Oh shit! Keith what's up?"

"Man, they bound me over as an adult. I'm in the county, my bond is $50,000. Ten percent of that is $5,000. I need you to get that to my mother as quick as possible. I need to get out, so that I can get me a lawyer. They don't really got shit on me. I didn't go in the store and none of y'all got caught. The only thing that is fucking me up is that they found some of the chains outside of the car. I need to get out though. Y'all get the money to my mother and she will handle it, y'all got me dawg?"

"For sure, we should have the money to your mother by tomorrow. Let me go find this nigga Bruce, so we can take care of it."

"Alright, I'm going to holla back tomorrow to see what's up."

"That's cool, holla at me my nigga." China Man told him, and then hung up. He got himself together, grabbed his car keys and headed out to find Bruce.

Ÿ

Dirty got to his aunt Lois' house and went inside. She was sitting in her kitchen playing cards with some of her friends. She looked up when Dirty entered the kitchen, "About damn time! What you forget you got a little brother, better yet you forgot you got family period. I haven't seen your big headed ass in months. I'm about to beat that little brother of yours ass if he don't get some act right about his self. You better talk to him," she yelled upstairs, "Dodee get your narrow ass down here!" Dodee came running down the stairs. When he got to the kitchen and seen Dirty standing there, he broke into a wide grin. He ran over to Dirty and wrapped his arms around him hugging him tightly.

"Come on, we are about to go for a ride," Dirty told him.

"I'll have him back before It gets too late," Dirty told Lois.

"He better have some sense when he gets back here too!" she yelled after them as they headed out of the door.

They got into Dirty's car and he pulled off. Dodee felt good riding with his brother.

"Is this your car?" he asked Dirty.

"Yeah, it's mine."

"Where are we going?"

"I'm taking you shopping."

"For real?"

"Yeah for real!"

"Now tell me this, why have you been giving aunt Lois so much trouble and fighting in school?" Dodee hunched his shoulders, "What the hell do that mean?" Dirty asked him.

"I don't know."

"What do you mean you don't know Dodee? There has got to be a reason for your behavior."

"I don't like it over there. I want to stay with you."

"You can't stay with me. I can't take care of you by myself. I'll tell you what, if you promise me that you are going to straighten up, I will talk Lois into letting you stay with me on the weekends. Can you do that?"

"Yeah, I can do that!"

"So, we got a deal right?"

"Yeah, we got a deal."

Dirty took Dodee downtown and bought him about ten outfits, two pair of tennis shoes and some socks, drawers and t-shirts. Then he took him to McDonald's, gave him fifty dollars, and then took him back to his aunt's house.

Dirty told Lois that he would be coming to get Dodee for the weekends and he also gave her two hundred dollars.

Ÿ

China Man went over to Bruce's house. Bruce had not been hanging out since he had got shot. He went out and bought him two pistols and was just sitting in the house waiting to heal all the way up, before he set out to get revenge.

He had started to smoke wet more frequently, which was taking him on a serious trip inside of his mind.

His sister Candy let China Man in. He went into the room, where Bruce was playing Nintendo. "What's good?" Bruce asked China Man when he stepped into the room.

"Shit, I just got a call from Keith. They bounded him over, and he is down in the county. He says he needs five thousand, so that he can get out on bond. What do you got on it?"

"Shit, I'm fucked up."

"Come on Bruce this our boy. I know you got something."

"I only got three thousand left to my name. All I can stand to give you is a thousand." China Man knew how selfish Bruce was. He put money before friendship. He was forgetting that even though Keith had gotten caught, he was still supposed to get a cut from the lick, but they hadn't put anything up for him. China Man felt bad about that.

He thought to himself, "Fuck it! I will put up four grand!" He felt that he owed Keith that, "Yeah man, give me the thousand." China man told him. Bruce went over to his dresser drawer and got a grand out of it and handed it to China Man.

"We got to hit another lick soon. I'm almost on empty!" Bruce told China Man.

"You holler at Dirty?"

"Nigga Dirty ain't fucking with you. We are going to hit one on our own again." Bruce was China Man's nigga, but China Man preferred to hit a lick with Dirty, because he knew that the lick would be well planned out and have a much bigger chance at success.

"I'll get at you tomorrow dawg. Hopefully Keith will be out by then." China Man told Bruce, then left.

Chapter 23

The next day Ron and Tim were called for attorney visits. They had their visits together even though they were codefendants, because they didn't have anything to hide from each other. The lawyers were a father and son team. Tom was the father and Burt was the son.

Tom told them that Mike had retained them to represent them, and that they were there to get their side of the story and to see how they wanted to proceed. They told them that after they heard what they had to say, they were going to see the prosecutor to get a discovery package.

Ron told them that there was only one witness. Some old lady that says she watched it from a window." Ron told Tom.

"If you find that you can't do shit for me, then I want you to concentrate on getting Tim off, because he did not do anything. Tom informed him that they were going to get with the prosecutor to see if they could work some things out, but that first they had to go over all of the evidence because there could be a possibility that they could get both Ron and Tim off. He told them that he and his son would be back in a couple of days.

Ron and Tim were escorted back to their pod. They were hype, "Damn that was fast!" Tim said to Ron.

"Yeah, he gave me his word, but I didn't think it would happen this quick. I got to get that punk ass counselor to give me a call." When they got back to their pod, Ron requested to see the counselor. The counselor called him out, "What is it now?"

"I need another call."

"1 just gave you a call yesterday."

"I know and I appreciate it. You know my situation and they are trying to bound me over and hit me with five to twenty five years. I'm trying to get my lawyer situation right."

"You got ten minutes."

"That's all I need, thanks." The counselor took Ron into his office and let him make a call. He called Mike and he answered, "What is up playboy?"

"How did you know it was me that was calling?"

"Cause I took care of my business and I been sitting by this phone all day waiting on you to call."

"Yeah, they came and seen us. They said they got to go holla at the prosecutor to see what all he got, before they know how to proceed."

"I told you that I had y'all. Y'all my niggas man, I been getting money, but it ain't been right without y'all. When y'all get out we are going to get with that nigga Dirty and hit a sweet lick. So you niggas hold on. I paid them lawyers five grand. If y'all need money on your books holla at me. Tell Tim I said I got him."

"Okay dawg, I got to go, but I'm going to get back up with you. You be easy out there one love!" Ron told him then hung up the phone. He went back to the pod feeling better. He thought that things might not turn out as bad as be first think they would.

Ÿ

The next day China Man took Keith's mother to a bondsman. She paid the bondsman and signed the paperwork. They went down to the county and waited for Keith to be released. When he came out and seen his mother and China Man standing there he broke out into a big smile.

He hugged his mother and gave China Man some dap. They all got in China Man's car and he drove out to the mall.

He took Keith shopping and got him some new gear and a couple pair of tennis shoes. Then he took Keith and his mother to the food court inside of the mall and got them something to eat. Afterwards, he took them home, where Keith took a shower then got dressed in some of the new gear that

China Man had gotten him. They left the house, with Keith promising his mother that he wouldn't be gone long.

China Man took Keith to his house and let him pick through his jewelry. Keith picked two gold nugget rings and a gold dookie rope.

They headed out and jumped back into China Man's car, "The nigga Vic shot Bruce huh?" Keith asked.

"Yeah, he shot him, I found out the whole truth behind that situation. That day Bruce shot dice against him, he lost all of his money and his car to Vic. He bucked on giving Vic the car and I guess Vic had somebody burn it up. Bruce caught him up in the plaza and beat the shit out of him, and Vic came back and shot him."

"Is he good?"

"Man, that nigga been smoking so much water, that he is starting to lose his mind. That nigga be all paranoid and shit, sitting up in the house with two guns." China Man wasn't going to tell Keith that Bruce only put up $1000.00 towards his bond. Keith thought that he and Bruce were tight, but China Man knew that they were not as tight as he thought.

"Take me to see him." Keith told him.

China Man drove over to Bruce house. Candy let them in and they walked back to Bruce's room and were overtaken by the smell of PCP.

Instead of knocking on his bedroom door, China Man just opened it. Bruce was lying on the bed getting some head from a girl that neither one of them had ever saw. When they entered the room the girl quickly pulled the cover up over her head.

Bruce seen who it was and pulled on his boxing shorts. He stood up and snatched the cover off of the girl, leaving her totally naked with her body exposed. The girl used her arms and hands to cover up what she could.

"These my niggas bitch and what's mines is theirs."

"You ain't got to hide from my niggas." he turned to Keith and said to him as he approached him and gave him a hug.

"Damn nigga! You done dipped your whole body in wet?" Keith asked him noticing how much Bruce smelled like PCP.

"I been hitting that butt naked nigga. It eases the pain from my bullet wounds. I know you heard that bitch ass nigga Vic shot me, I got something for that nigga's ass though!" Bruce told Keith.

He walked over to his dresser and pulled two black forty fives out of the drawer.

"Yeah that nigga a dead man walking!" Bruce said then left the guns on top of the dresser. "Forget all that my nigga, you're fresh out. You want some head or something?" Keith looked at the girl curled up on the bed. She was cute and had a fat ass.

"Nigga you want some head from the bitch or what?" Bruce asked him again.

"You tripping!"

"Nigga I ain't tripping, I'm pimping. Monica come give my nigga some head bitch! You smoked up a sixty five dollar bottle of water, you got to work that shit off. This nigga is fresh out of the county. Give my nigga some of that skull, so he can get some release."

Monica slowly got up off of the bed and approached Keith. She walked towards him like a zombie. She got in front of him and dropped down to her knees. She unzipped his pants, pulled his dick out and started sucking it right there in front of Bruce and China Man with no shame whatsoever.

Keith and China Man were both amazed. "Let the nigga do his thing." Bruce told China Man as he opened the door to exit the room. China Man went up to the living room and Bruce went into the bathroom to take a shower.

Back in the bedroom Monica was sucking the skin off of Keith's dick, but it did nothing for him. He had been in the county for months and wanted some pussy.

"Get up and get on the bed doggy style." he told the girl. She did as she was told and Keith dropped his pants and drawers to the floor. He fucked her doggy style until he came. He wiped his dick off on her ass, and then pulled his clothes back up.

Monica picked the cover up off of the floor, crawled back onto the bed and pulled the cover up over her covering her whole body including her head.

Keith left out of the room and went up to the living room with China Man.

Bruce finished his shower, went back into his room and got dressed. He grabbed his two guns off of the dresser and left out of his bedroom closing the door behind him. He did not say one word to Monica. He went into the living room, "Come on y'all." He told them. They got off of the couch and followed him out the door.

"Let's take my car." Bruce told them wanting to show Keith how he was riding. Keith notice that Bruce was walking with a slight limp.

"You limping, is you good dawg?" Keith asked him.

"Yeah, I'm good, I'm going to dead that bitch ass nigga when I catch him."

Keith started seeing what China Man had been telling him. Bruce had changed, his personality and attitude was different. He thought that the wet must have been taking a toll on him.

They got in Bruce's Audi. He drove up to the plaza and copped a forty ounce from the beverage store. When he came out of the store he scanned the plaza for any sign of Vic. After not seeing any, he got back in the car and pulled around to the courts, so that everybody could see that Keith was out.

They got up there and the street was roped off, they had to park at the top of the street, get out and walk. They were having a block party at the courts. They had Bar-B-Q grills set up all around. Music was blaring. Little kids ran around eating watermelon.

"Damn nigga, it's like they knew that you were getting out today!" Bruce told him laughing. They joined the festivities. Bruce jumped into a dice game, while Keith and China Man shot basketball.

Chapter 24

Dirty, Rab and George were chilling at Dirty's house. Robin was upstairs sleep. Dirty took notice that Robin had been sleeping a lot recently.

They were sitting in the living room going over the next lick that they were to hit, "I wanted to hit a lick out in PA, but my connect couldn't get me enough information to go on, so we are going to hit a jewelry store inside of Randall Mall."

"You want to hit a jewelry store inside of Randall Park Mall?" asked George.

"Yep! My source told me that their security ain't as tight as everybody thinks. All it's going to take is a screwdriver and a couple of those pellets. We are going to hit it late at night, when the mall is closed. It's a air vent that leads directly inside of JB Robinson's jewelry store. We go in, hit the cases and jet."

"It can't be that simple Dirty." Rab stated.

"Rab, sometimes the things that seem so simple be the hardest things to do, and sometimes things that seem so hard to do really be easy. I'm going to holla at Bruce and Mike because we need a couple extra people. Plus we need some of them pellets that Mike be having.

We are going for it this weekend. Sometime this week I am going out there to time the security patrols. Right now I got to bounce I got somebody to meet."

They all got up and left. Rab jumped on his scooter while George got in his Lac and Dirty got into his Camaro.

Dirty headed down to the Marriot Hotel, down on East 30th and Euclid. When he got there, he headed upstairs to the seventh floor and looked for room 717. He located it near the end of the hall on his left side.

Dirty knocked on the door and it opened, Mary, Hobo's mother stood there wearing nothing but a red teddy and matching panties. Dirty's eyes damn near bulged out of their sockets as he looked at her big, dark nipples poking through the fabric.

"Are you just going to stand there or are you going to come in?" Mary asked him breaking the spell that she had him up under.

Dirty entered the room and stood by the door. Mary closed the door then went and sat on the bed with her legs gapped open. Dirty had to cough to clear his throat, "I thought you said you wanted to meet me so that we can talk about some business?"

"No, I said that I needed to meet with you so that we could handle some business." Mary told him seductively.

"Listen Mary, you cool and all, but me and Hobo are alright. I don't want to fall out with him."

"Dirty I'm a grown woman. Don't I look grown to you?" Mary asked him as she stood up, pulled the teddy up over her head then stepped out of her panties.

Dirty just stood there staring at her pussy which had a bush as thick as a forest. He looked to her stomach, which was flat as a board and her titties which sat high up on her chest without a bra.

"Dirty, my son has no problem with who I fuck. I would not cause problems within my family. You are special, you may be young, but you are beyond your years. Let me take you places that you have never been before."

Mary grabbed Dirty's hand and led him over to the bed. She unbuttoned his shirt and helped him out of it. She undid his pants, and Dirty kicked his shoes off so that they could get his pants and drawers off. He stood there in his socks, "I need those off too baby." Mary told him.

She sat down on the bed in front of him and looked him over from head to toe. She liked everything about him, his dark Hershey bar complexion, his perfectly formed chest, and his six pack stomach. What she liked most, was his dick.

Dirty's dick stood up as if it was saluting someone. Instead of sticking straight out, it stood straight up, and it reached past his navel, and was thick as a man's wrist.

"You are a very fine specimen, you are so beautiful." Mary told him as she reached out and grabbed his dick. Her soft manicured hands, sent shivers through Dirty. She bent her head down and took one of his balls into her mouth. She sucked on it as she massaged the other one, "Ummm!" she moaned as she switched from one to the other.

When she got through sucking his balls she blew on them. He felt a cool sensation as her hot breath hit the saliva that she left on his dick and started to dry it. Next she spit on the head of his dick and engulfed it.

She did not just suck Dirty's dick, she made love to it. Dirty did something that he had never done before, he pushed Mary's head off of his dick. His dick had become too sensitive to the pleasure that she was giving him. It was like having his feet tickled.

Little did he know Mary was just getting started. Mary did many things to Dirty that night that no other woman had ever done before. She kissed and licked him from head to toe. She nibbled on his ears, licked the spine of his back, nibbled on his nipples. She even licked the crack of his ass and sucked his balls from the back.

Dirty did not know if he should feel flattered or angry after the things that Mary had done to him.

He did not know if it was right to let her do some of the things that she had done to him, like blowing into and licking his ass. She even had the nerve to sit on his face and grind her pussy on it until she came. Dirty started choking when some of her cum got in his nose and went down the back of his throat.

Dirty knew one thing for sure, that the time he spent with Mary that night, would never be forgotten.

When they were finished sexing they took a shower together and Mary washed him from head to toe. They got out of the shower, got dressed and parted ways.

Dirty felt guilty about what he had done and decided not to go home to Robin. He instead, headed to Tonya's house. He figured that since she was eight months pregnant that she wouldn't press him for any sex. His dick was too sensitive to go another round. He got there and crashed on her coach.

Chapter 25

Bruce, China Man and Keith were up in the Omens. After they left the cookout, they went home showered and changed clothes. China Man drove his car, following Bruce and Keith up to the Omens. They made a pit stop in King Kennedy, where Bruce bought a wet joint, and then they headed to the club.

When they first got down there it was still early, so they just stayed outside and mingled with people in the parking lot. When the club started getting packed they decided to go in.

They were up in the Omens getting praised. They were geared and draped up and had knots of money in their pockets. China Man and Keith were just vibing, putting their mack down on the girls.

Bruce was high walking through the club tripping. He was looking at people and mumbling to himself.

He peeped somebody that looked familiar to him, as he walked through the crowd, "Bitch ass nigga, I knew I would run into you!" he said to his self.

He went to find China Man and Keith. He found them over in a corner posted up against the wall talking to some chicks.

"We got to go y'all!" he told them.

"What's up Bruce?" China Man asked him with an irritated expression on his face.

"We got some business to handle."

"You tripping man, we supposed to be chilling tonight." Keith told him.

"Y'all don't want to get this money with me, fuck y'all then!" Bruce told them then walked off.

"Man, that nigga just high, he will be all right." China Man told Keith.

Bruce stalked the person that he recognized until it looked like he was getting ready to leave. Bruce hurried up and exited the club. He went to his car and grabbed his two pistols. He stood off in the shadows until he seen the person come out of the club.

The person that he was waiting for came out. He was dressed in a Gucci suit and shoes and carried a Gucci pouch in his hand. The figure crossed the street, and Bruce started to trail him. He ducked behind cars so that he wouldn't be seen.

The figure approached a triple black Cadillac Fleetwood that had gold emblems on it. The person that he was following walked around to the back of the car and stuck a key into the trunk's lock.

"I knew I would catch your bitch ass!" Bruce said to the person's back. The figure turned around and immediately recognized Bruce, who had two forty fives pointed at his chest. "You ain't still tripping over that bullshit, is you?"

"Nigga, you owe me drop down." Lou tried to talk his way out of it, "Come on baby, I played fair with y'all, I put money in y'all's pockets."

"I ain't trying to hear that shit! Break yourself before I make you eat these bullets!" Lou dropped his pouch and went to reach inside of his pants. Bruce tripping off the wet thought that Lou was reaching for a pistol and started unloading on him with both guns. He hit Lou fourteen times before he fell, and six afterwards. He tucked his guns into his waist, bent over and started going through Lou's pockets. He took knots of money out of both of Lou's pockets, and then stripped him of his jewelry.

He picked up the Gucci pouch and seen that it was full of small bottles of wet. Bruce seen that the keys were still sticking in the trunk. He decided that he would stuff Lou's body into the trunk so that no one would see him. He turned the key and the trunk popped opened.

When the trunk opened, its lights came on and Bruce seen that a lot of what looked to be gallon jugs lined the trunks floor. He picked up one of the jugs and put it up to his nose and sniffed it. The smell of PCP filled

Bruce's nostrils. Bruce knew that it was wet. He started pulling the jugs out of the trunk and sitting them on the ground. It was seven gallon jugs altogether. Once he had the trunk clear, he lifted Lou's body up, pushed it into the trunk then closed it. He used his shirt to wipe his prints off of the keys and off of the trunk's lock.

He made three trips to his car, carrying the gallons of water. He put the gallons into his trunk and headed home. He had seven gallons of PCP, with each gallon being worth $35,000 to $50,000. He hit the lick all by himself, so he did not have to split the money with anyone. If Bruce played his cards right he would be straight for life.

China Man and Keith left out of the club with the two girls and seen that Bruce car was gone. They decided to take the girls to the hotel.

Chapter 26

Dirty sat in his car, over in Radio Shack's parking lot which sat across the street from the mall. He sat there timing the mall's security guards making their rounds. He had seen that they made rounds every thirty minutes. Dirty knew that they would have to work east, and that they would not be able to park inside of the mall's parking lot.

They were going to have to park somewhere else and walk to the mall. Dirty pulled out of the parking lot and drove around the area looking for a place to park. He came across a spot that was heavily lined with trees, but through the trees he could see an apartment complex.

Dirty turned down a street and drove a little ways. He came upon the apartment complex and pulled in it. He pulled into the back of the complex and seen the woods behind it. He put his car in park, got out and walked to the wooded area. When he got there he seen what looked to be a bike trail, and followed it. It ended the sidewalk, which was right across the street from the mall.

"Bingo!" Dirty said to his self.

He had found the getaway route. He decided that the next day, he would go holla at Bruce and Mike, and then he drove home.

When he went into the house, Robin was sitting on the living room couch with a big smile on her face, "What are you in such a good mood about?" Dirty asked her.

"Guess!"

"Robin, I ain't trying to play twenty one questions right now, what's up?"

"I'm pregnant!"

"You're what?"

"I'm pregnant!" Robin told him cheesing.

Dirty did not know how to take what she was telling him. He did not know if he could handle her losing another baby, "How far along are you?"

"I'm seven weeks."

"Do you think it is wise for you to be pregnant again?"

"What do you mean?" Robin asked him starting to feel down.

"I mean you lost the last one, who's to say that you won't lose this one?"

"I got a prenatal doctor, and she gave me a full checkup. He told me that I was fine and gave me the green light to proceed with the pregnancy. He gave me some vitamins and put me on a dietary diet. I will see her twice a month for checkups. I'm going to have this baby Dirty. I'm going to be your baby's mother!" Robin did not know that dirty had another girl pregnant and that she was almost due to have the baby.

Dirty knew that he faced difficult times ahead, but that he needed to stay focused on the upcoming lick. The lick that could set him straight for life.

He went over to Robin, hugged her and told her, "I love you," they then went upstairs made love and fell asleep in each other's arms.

Ÿ

The next morning Bruce was out and about. He was spreading the word that he had the water. He went up to Bundy drive and tried to sell water to the hustlers. They waved him off, so he set up shop and started under cutting them. He sold water at half the price that the hustlers in King Kennedy were selling it for. To top it off his wet was uncut. When the hustlers seen that all the customers were going to Bruce they were forced to start dealing with him.

He told them that he had anything from joints to gallons. Within two hours Bruce had made over ten thousand dollars.

He left King Kennedy and pulled down to the courts. China Man and Keith were up there. They walked up to Bruce car after he parked. Bruce got out and they noticed that he had on new jewelry, including a presidential Rolex watch.

"Where did you go last night?" China man asked him.

"I hit a lick for over seven gallons of water, fifteen thousand cash and this jewelry."

"You're lying!" China Man said not believing that he had hit a lick for that much.

"If I'm lying, I'm flying baby boy. I'm set for life! No more lick hitting for me."

"Put your boys on dawg!" Keith said to him all hype.

"Yeah right, you niggas chose some broke ass bitches over getting money last night. I had to get blood on my hands and you niggas were nowhere around. Now you want me to give y'all something."

"You tripping Bruce!" Keith told him. Before Bruce could respond, they heard a car horn. They all turned around and seen that it was Dirty.

Dirty got out of his car and approached them, "What's good y'all," he said as he reached his hand out to give them some dap. He gave Bruce and Keith some dap. He pulled his hand back when China Man tried to give him some dap.

"Dirty, you still tripping off of that bullshit. I was wrong dawg that was my bad."

"We alright, we just can't do anything together anymore." He turned to Bruce, "A Bruce let me holla at you for a minute." him and Bruce walked off together, leaving China Man and Keith standing there, "What's up Dirty?" Bruce asked him.

"I got a lick set up! It's sweet and we can get more than we got last time. I just need two more people to make my team complete, I was thinking about you and Mike, do you want in?"

"Dirty, I'm out of the hittin' lick business, my nigga. I hit a lick that's going to set me straight for life. I got seven gallons of clicker juice. I'm about to do my thing. Keith will be down for sure. That nigga is fresh out of the county trying to get   money for a lawyer."

Dirty took note that Bruce had just told him that he had hit a lick that was going to set him straight for life, yet he wasn't putting his boy on.

"Call Keith over here,"

"A Keith, come here right quick!" Bruce yelled out to him. Keith walked over to them, "Dirty got a lick set up, and he said that he needs a couple more people. He wanted me, but I told him you can take my spot if you want it!"

"Hell yeah, I will take it!"

"It's going down Saturday night, so I'm going to pick you up about seven, is that cool?"

"I'll be ready my nigga."

"Wear some dark clothing too, no bright colors."

"I got you!"

"You say that you got that clicker Bruce, fire up one with me," Dirty told him.

"No doubt, let's go to my car." Bruce replied and started heading towards his car. When they got into the car Dirty asked Bruce if he had a pen. Bruce told him to look inside of the glove compartment.

While Dirty looked for a pen, Bruce pulled out a bottle that was filled with wet joints. He took one out and fired it up.

Dirty found a pen, then tore a piece off of a match book cover and wrote his pager number down. He handed it to Bruce and told him to give it to Mike and tell him to page him.

They sat there and smoked the joint until it was gone, "This shit is full proof!" Dirty said to Bruce.

"It's that clicker my nigga ain't no cut on this. It sends niggas up to Captain Kirk."

"Sale me two sticks."

"Nigga, I'll give you two sticks. Fuck I look like charging you for this shit and you put me on." Bruce pulled two wet sticks out of the bottle and handed them to Dirty. "You sure you're good on this lick?" Dirty asked him.

"Yeah, I'm sure my nigga. I'm going to work this water."

"Suit yourself." Dirty told him then got out of the car. Dirty got in his car and pulled off driving five miles per hour. Drivers honked their horns trying to get Dirty to speed up, but ended up having to pull around him.

Dirty wasn't even aware that he was only driving five miles per hour as he headed to Tonya's house. When he got there, he threw up all over her living room floor, and then fell asleep on her couch.

Chapter 27

Tom and Burt went back to see Ron and Tim. Tom told them, "Here is the deal, that old woman is senile. I believe that we can discredit her. She never seen you throw anything through the window, and she never seen you attempt to reach inside of the car. It's going to be tough, but if you can have your friend come up with five more thousand dollars, I think I could get both of you guys to walk." Ron and Tim got hyped, "Are you serious?" asked Ron.

"As serious as the heart attack that the lady had."

"It's a done deal." Ron told him banking on Mike to put up the money for them.

"Well as soon as he gets the money to me, I can start working on getting you guys out of here." They ended the visit and Ron and Tim were taken back to their pod.

When Ron got back, he played for another call from his counselor. The counselor gave him a call and he called Mike. Mike's mother answered the phone. She asked Ron how he was doing then handed the phone to Mike, "What's up playboy?"

"Look, the lawyers just left from seeing me and Tim. They told us that for five thousand more dollars that they can get us both to walk."

"I ain't got it right now, but I just hollered at Dirty earlier and he got a lick set up for Saturday, so I should have the money by at least Tuesday or Wednesday."

"But you got us right?"

"I got y'all baby boy. Soon as I get rid of some of the shit, I'm going to shoot them ends to the lawyers."

"That's a bet my nigga. I'm going to try to call Sunday to see if everything went good."

"That's cool,"

"Alright one!" Ron told him, and then hung up.

Ÿ

Saturday came, and Dirty was up bright and early. Him and Robin went and picked up Dodee. Dirty took both of them shopping and out to get something to eat. At four o'clock he took them to the house, and then headed down the way. He knew that he was early. He had told Keith seven o'clock, but to his surprise when he pulled up to the courts Keith was up there sitting on a bench watching a basketball game.

Dirty blew his horn and Keith looked up. He seen Dirty and got up and headed to his car. He climbed, into the front seat, "If you had a job, you would never get fired for being late," Dirty told him laughing.

"It's all about the paper." Keith responded.

"I know that's right." Dirty pulled around the corner to Mike's house and blew the horn. Mike came out bopping, and climbed into Dirty's backseat, "What's good y'all?" he asked them.

Dirty told Mike, "I'm about to shoot over to the west side. I need you to steal two four door cars. You can drive one and Keith can drive the other one."

"Let's go!" Mike told him.

"You got the pellets right?" Dirty asked him.

"For sure." he handed Dirty the pellets.

Dirty headed out to the Westgate Mall and Mike peeled two columns of a Chevy and a Bonneville.

They followed Dirty back over to the east side and up to Rab's house. George and Rab were there waiting.

They all went down into the basement to go over the plan one last time. Dirty started explaining it, "Rab, you are going to drive one car, and Mike you are going to drive the other one. George me and you are going in and

Keith, you are going to be the lookout. You are going to stay inside of the vent and watch out for security patrols. We are going to park the cars in a apartment complex and walk through some woods over to the mall. The security makes its rounds every half an hour, so we have to move quickly. We have to get the vent open, get into the store, get the shit, and get back out all within a half an hour. Now, is there any questions?"

"Is it going to be hard to get the vent open?"

"I got a power drill in my bag along with some WD40 oil, in case the screws are rusted, so there shouldn't be a problem, any more questions? Okay then, we got a couple of hours before we move, so we might as well chill here," Dirty told them.

They all started playing games, George and Rab played ice hockey, and Mike and Keith shot pool while Dirty played the Pac Man game.

At ten o'clock, they all headed out to the cars. Rab got into the driver's side of the Chevy and George and Keith climbed in with him. Dirty chose to ride in the Bonneville with Mike. Mike was the lead car and Dirty directed him out to the housing complex. When they entered it, they pulled into the back they couldn't find parking spots right next to each other. They had to park four spots over from one another. They backed into the parking spots.

Dirty got out of the car with a gym bag in his hand as George and Keith joined him, "Y'all ready?" Dirty asked them. They both shook their heads and Dirty led the way through the wooded area. They crouched down when they came to the end of the wooded area and watched the mall.

Fifteen minutes later a little white security car came circling around the mall's parking lot. They sat and watched the car drive all the way around the mall then pull out of the lot.

"Come on y'all!' Dirty told them as he stood up and walked out of the woods. They jogged across the street and through the mall's parking lot. Dirty led them to Joseph Horne's department store and right next to it down by the ground was a vent. The vent had a cover that was secured by six screws.

"Y'all watch out!" Dirty told them as he knelt down by the vent. He opened up the gym bag and pulled out the WD40. He sprayed oil on all of the screws, and then he reached into the bag and pulled out a battery operated screwdriver.

He easily removed the screws from the vent's cover, "Keith come help me pull the cover off!" Dirty called out to him. Keith went over and knelt on the other side of Dirty. Together they wedged the cover off of the vent and sat it on the ground. "Come on George!" Dirty called to him. George knelt down and crawled into the vent. Next Dirty crawled in, with Keith following him. Dirty and Keith pulled the cover back up to the vent, "Just hold onto it, and stay on the lookout!" Dirty told him.

Dirty and George proceeded through the vent until they came to the end. There was another vent cover securing it from the outside. Dirty knew that he would not be able to unscrew the screws from the inside of the vent, so he had brought an electric battery operated drill. He pulled the drill out of the bag and drilled the screws out. After they were out, he used his feet to kick the cover off.

Dirty stuck his head out of the vent and seen that it led into an office. He climbed out of the vent, and then pulled the bag out. George followed him out of the vent.

Dirty opened the office door and broke out smiling as he stared into the jewelry store. He had seen display case after display case full of jewelry. George looked and seen what Dirty was smiling about and they started giving each other dap.

Dirty pulled another bag out of the gym bag and handed it to George. Then he handed him some pellets. "Find the cases with the most expensive shit in them and hit them!" Dirty told George, then they went to work.

Ÿ

Back over at the apartment complex Rab and Mike were sitting in the cars, when they seen headlights entering the complex. Rab thought quick and laid down on the seat. Mike stayed sitting up and the next thing he knew there was a bright light shining in his face. A security car equipped with a side light was making rounds through the parking lot shining the light on all the cars as it drove by. The security guard had seen Mike sitting in the car. He looked like a deer that was caught in some headlights late at night. The security guard continued on making his rounds.

He took notice that he was a young black male being out there in a white neighborhood that late at night. He pulled out of the lot of the complex but parked across the street from it and cut off his lights. He was going to wait to see what was up with that car.

Ÿ

Back at the mall in the vent, Keith felt like he was starting to hyperventilate. He fell to tell Dirty that he was claustrophobic, when Dirty asked them if they had anything to say. It started becoming hard for him to breathe. He decided that he would get out of the vent for a minute, just to get a little fresh air. He pushed the cover off of the vent and crawled out. He put the vent cover back in place and stood up.

He took deep breaths trying to relax. Before he knew what was going on, he was standing in front of a pair of headlights. The mall's security guard had decided to make another round. The guard pulled on the side of Keith and asked him, "What are you doing?"

"I'm waiting on the bus."

"You're waiting on the bus?"

"Yeah, I walked down here from Southgate to catch the 19 downtown."

"What were you doing at Southgate?"

"I was at the movies."

"Okay, well the bus does not come onto the mall's property after ten o'clock. You are going to have to stand out on the main street down by Arby's restaurant."

"Okay, thank you officer." Keith told him as he started walking. The officer drove slowly watching to make sure that Keith left the property. Once Keith was off the property the guard decided, to make another round to make sure that there wasn't anyone else on the property.

Ÿ

Dirty and George had broken into six cases and filled the bags up, "Man, we can't leave all of this shit!" Damn, we should have brung more people." George said.

"Fuck it let's stuff our pockets and socks!" Dirty said then broke another case. They started stuffing jewelry into their front pockets, back pockets and their socks, "Let's go!" Dirty told George. They headed back into the office and climbed back into the vent. They crawled to the end and seen that Keith wasn't there, "Fuck is this nigga at!" Dirty said heatedly.

"This shit is crazy! All Bruce people are fucked up!" George stated.

Dirty pushed the vent open and crawled out. He pulled the two bags out of the vent, and then George climbed out, "you putting the cover back on?" George asked Dirty.

"Fuck that, let's go!" They headed across the lot toting the bags. It was difficult walking with jewelry stuffed into their pockets and socks.

They got to the middle of the lot, when the security guard came circling back around the block. He seen Dirty and George toting the heavy bags and sped in their direction. The roar of an engine caused Dirty and George to turn around. They see a little white security car coming their way.

"Oh shit! Go!" Dirty said and took off running. They made it to the sidewalk. The security guard had to get out of the lot through the exit to pursue them. As he raced towards the exit, he radioed in for back up. Dirty and George ran across the street and headed into the woods. The security guard gave dispatch the direction that they ran in. The security guard that was parked outside of the complex heard the call go out over the radio, and figured that he had them.

They came out of the woods and George jumped into the car with Rab, but they did not pull right out waiting to see if Keith was going to come. Dirty jumped into the car with Mike and Mike sped out of the lot. As soon as he pulled out the security guard pulled out behind them. George told Rab, "Fuck it go that nigga wasn't there!" Rab pulled out of the lot and turned to head in the direction that they had come but up ahead he seen lights on top of a car, "Shit! That's the police up there!" Rab said.

"Turn this bitch around!" George told him. Rab busted a U-turn and headed in the other direction. He came out on Warrensville Center Road and seen the freeway. He headed towards it and got on it.

The security guard radioed in the plates of the car and the direction that it was going in. The dispatcher notified the security guard that the car was stolen and that, they were now inside of Cleveland so the CPD had been notified.

Mike was driving down Miles Road, when he got to the intersection at Lee Road they were cut off from every direction by the Cleveland Police Department. Mike threw the car in reverse and tried to back up but was rear ended by the security car.

The police officers jumped out of their cars with guns drawn and ordered them to shut the car off and get out with their hands in the air. The police approached them and searched them. They found all types of jewelry in Dirty's pockets and socks. They searched the car and found a bag full of jewelry and tools, "Oh shit! They must have broken into the mall!" one of the officers yelled out to the others.

"Send some cars up to the mall to check it out," Some officers jumped into their cars and headed up to the mall. The security guard that had first spotted them was the closest and he went into the parking lot and circled it until he came across the vent cover lying on the ground.

Keith seen Dirty and George get chased while he stood at the bus stop. A bus had yet to come, so he took off walking. Two police cruisers on their way to the mall had seen him. They stopped and called him over to the car. He went to them and they asked him what he was doing out there that time of night. He gave them the same excuse that he had given the guard, only they didn't go for it they quickly jumped out and placed him in the back of one of the cruisers.

They wanted the guard to get a chance to see if he was one of the ones that fled the scene. They continued on to the mall. When they entered its parking lot they went in the direction of all the flashing lights that they see. There were eight police officers and four security guards standing next to a hole in the side of the wall. There was a metal vent cover lying on the ground next to the hole.

"Did y'all get them?" the guard asked them.

"We apprehended two suspects that had plenty of jewelry on them. Then we picked up a fella walking around on our way up here. We would like for you to take a look at him. to see if he was one of them."

The guard followed the officer to the back of his patrol car. The guard looked into the back seat, "That there fella is the first one that I see on the property. He told me that he was waiting on the bus. He was standing in this area too, he could of been the lookout."

"Yeah, well he will be looking out of a cell window tonight, we are taking him in." Even though the Cleveland police had apprehended all of them, the crime had been committed in Warrensville, so they had to take all the suspects to North Randall jail.

Dirty, Mike and Keith were all booked for burglary and aggravated robbery, and then put in a cell.

Chapter 28

Rab and George made it safely back to Rab's house. They put the jewel-ry up, then George jumped into his car and followed Rab to go get rid of the stolen car.

They went back to Rab's house to wait on a call from Dirty. They thought that maybe it was a chance that he had gotten away. They did not even mess with the jewelry. Rab just put the bag into his bedroom closet. They fell asleep waiting on Dirty to call.

Ÿ

Monday, Dirty, Mike and Keith went before a judge, and were given half a million dollar bonds. They were told that they would have to sit in North Randall's jail until they had a preliminary hearing, which was scheduled for ten days later.

When they got back to the city jail, they all got to use the phone. The first person that Dirty called was Robin. He told her what had happened and what jail he was in. He told her to come out there and see him. Next, he called Rab's house. Rab heard the phone ring and rushed   to pick it up.

He heard the operator say, "You have a collect call from Tyrone, do you accept the call?"

"Yeah, I accept," said Rab, who then yelled to George and told him that Dirty was on the phone. The call was put through, "Dirty what happened? We had been waiting to hear from you for two days."

"We got popped and it's all bad! They gave us half a million dollar bonds. Listen I want you and George to go up to Hobo's store and tell him I said for him to call his mother for y'all, because y'all got something for her. Whatever y'all get just split it up and put our cuts up. We can't get bond, but we are going to need to hire some lawyers."

"What else do you want us to do?"

"We will talk about it later, when I get down to the county. Just take care of that for right now."

"Okay we got you dawg." Dirty hung up and went back to his cell.

George and Rab went up to Hobo's store and had him call his mother. While they were waiting for her to get there Hobo shot his pitch at Rab. He took him into the back of the store and showed him a box that was full of kilos of cocaine.

He told Rab, "I tried to tell Dirty before he got caught up, that this is the way to go. It's quicker and easier money. I will let you get one for twenty five and I will teach you everything that you need to learn about the business. It sales itself, so just think about it, and when you are ready holla at me."

"Alright," Rab told him. Mary came and they told her what happened. She instantly felt disappointed when she heard the news about Dirty. She liked Dirty and was looking forward to seeing him when she got to the store.

"What do y'all got?" she asked them. They showed her the gym bag, which had over $600,000 worth of jewelry in it.

She took them to Marty's and made them wait in the car. They waited for about an hour, before she came out. She came out with $250,000. She took her $2,500 commission and handed them $247,500.

"They headed back to Rab's house and split the money up five ways. They got thirty five thousand apiece.

Rab stuffed Dirty, Mike and Keith's money back into the bag and put it back into the closet. George and Rab each left the house. Rab jumped on his scooter and headed up to Hobo's store. Hobo seen him come through the door and smiled. Rab walked up to the counter and dropped a sack of money on it, "Let me get one of them things."

"Come on into the back!" Rab followed him into the back of the store, "Before I give it to you I got to show you some things." Hobo took Rab into his office and taught him how to measure dope by the eye, how to weigh it on the scale. He taught him how to cut it and bag it up. He also showed him the different sizes, twenties, fifties and hundreds.

It took Hobo an hour and a half to teach him everything. When he was through, he gave Rab a kilo of coke, and he gave him a pocket scale. Rab got on his scooter and headed back on to begin his new hustle.

Ÿ

Bruce had been killing them with the water. Word had spread throughout the city quickly that he had the best water in the city, and since Lou wasn't anywhere to be found, lots of people needed a connect.

Bruce had gone through three gallons in five days. He had four gallons left. The only problem that he had was that he kept increasing the amount of water that he smoked his self.

Bruce would start his day off, by smoking a wet stick. That morning he did the same routine, smoked a wet stick, and then headed up to the courts.

He got up there and parked his car. China Man pulled in behind him, got out of his car and walked up to Bruce's car and got in.

"You know that Keith keeps calling telling me to ask you to get him out on bond."

"That nigga is crazy, if he thinks I'm putting up a half a million for him to get out. That nigga better wait that shit out."

"Aye you remember that nigga Lou that you said played you and Dirty?"

"What about him?"

"They found that nigga dead inside the trunk of his car. His car had gotten towed to the impound and they say after four days a bad smell started coming from the trunk. The workers busted the trunk open and found his body inside."

"That's fucked up! Karma is a bitch!" Bruce said as he pulled out another wet stick and lit it. He started his car up and pulled off, "Nigga where are you going?" China Man asked him.

"Up to the plaza to get a beer." Bruce continued to smoke the wet as he drove.

He pulled into the plaza's parking lot and seen that it was a dice game going on. He parked in front of the beverage store and reached under his seat and pulled out the same two forty fives that he had killed Lou with.

"What you need them for?" China Man asked him.

"Just in case I see that bitch ass nigga," Bruce got out of the car and went into the store. He bought a forty ounce, then headed out of the store and down towards the dice game.

China Man got out of the car and followed behind Bruce to make sure that he did not get into anything. He was back to far to intervene though. As soon as Bruce heard Vic's voice say what the hit for, he dropped the forty ounce and pulled out the two guns. When people heard the bottle shatter on the ground they turned and seen Bruce standing there with two guns in his hand. They broke out running and yelling, "He got a gun!"

Vic seen all the commotion and tried to reach for a gun that he had in his waist. He pulled it out, but before he could raise it, he was lifted off of his feet, when two slugs from the forty five hit him in his chest. When he fell to the ground the pistol that he had in his hand fell to the ground also. Bruce advanced on him.

"Bruce! Don't!" China Man yelled to him. Bruce stood over Vic, who was coughing up blood. He was lying on his back looking up at the sky, "What's up now nigga?" Bruce asked Vic as he struggled for breath, "Cat got your tongue? Maybe these will help you my nigga." Bruce unloaded the rest of the bullets from both guns into Vic's body.

"Shit!" China Man said to his self as he took off running. He ran all the way to Bruce house and banged on the door. Candy opened the door ready to cuss him out for banging on the door like that. She seen the look on China Man's face and knew something was wrong.

"Candy Bruce just killed Vic up in the plaza!"

"What!"

"He shot Vic, I know he's dead." Candy took off running out of the door. China Man went into Bruce room and opened his closet. He had seen the four gallons of water. He took a pillow case off of a pillow and put the jugs into it and left the house.

After Bruce killed Vic, he calmly walked back into the beverage store with the guns still in his hands and bought another forty ounce. The store clerk was scared to death, thinking that Bruce was going to rob the store, but he placed two dollars on the counter and exited the store.

Bruce got in his car, cracked the forty open, then pulled off. By the time he got to the stoplight four police cars were behind him.

Candy had just got to the corner and seen what was going on. She watched as the police followed Bruce with their lights flashing and sirens blaring.

Bruce continued to drive normal. He was so high that he didn't even comprehend what was going on around him.

He turned onto 43rd and headed back up to the courts. Candy seen the direction that he was going in and knew that he was heading to the courts she took off running as fast as she could towards the courts.

Bruce pulled to the curb in front of the courts. He pulled out another wet joint and lit it. He sat there in the car smoking it as the police cleared the area. They cleared everyone off of the basketball court and from around the immediate area.

SWAT was called in and snipers were set up. All of a sudden Bruce's car door opened and he stepped out of the car holding the forty ounce in one hand and one of the forty fives in the other. The officers all took cover. The head of the SWAT team got on the bull horn and kept telling Bruce to drop the gun. Bruce was so high that he could not comprehend what was going on. He started walking in the direction of the officers, "Stop! Stop now!" The officer yelled at Bruce. When Bruce got too close the officer felt that he had no choice but to give the signal. Candy was almost there and she seen the standoff. "Bruce!" she yelled as she tried to get there, but it was too late the SWAT commander gave the signal and they started unloading on Bruce.

Bruce was shot twenty seven times. Candy watched in horror as her brother went down in a hail of bullets. Bruce was dead before his body hit the ground.

Chapter 29

Seven days later, Bruce was laid to rest. On that same day Dirty, Keith and Mike went to their preliminary hearing. Rab had taken ten thousand dollars out of each of their cuts and hired them attorneys.

Dirty and Mike were bound over to the grand jury. The charges against Keith were dropped, because there was no evidence linking him to them or the crime. He had missed a court appearance for the case that he was out on bond on, so a warrant had been issued for his arrest and his bond had been revoked. He was transported down to the county along with Dirty and Mike. Rab took the rest of his cut to his mother and he eventually paid a new bond and got released.

China Man attended Bruce's funeral. When the funeral was over, he left jumping into his new BMW and headed to the wet strip which he had taken over. He did do a good deed of covering the cost of Bruce's funeral. He felt that it was the least that he could do for someone, whose tragedy became his blessing.

Ÿ

Rab turned the weed strip into a dope strip, and within weeks he was selling weight. George had seen how much money that Rab was making and decided to partner up with him. They became the first two young niggas out of Garden Valley to blow up. They opened up a club, a barber shop and bought many houses. They also put money aside for Dirty. They were going to make sure that when he got out that he would be straight.

Mike stayed a man of his word. Even with his troubles, he still had Rab give the five thousand dollars to the lawyers, for Ron and Tim. After his own lawyer fees and helping out his boys he had about ten thousand dollars left that Rab took to his mother. He told his mother to keep half for her and put the other half on his books.

Ron and Tim both walked free on their charges. They hooked up with China Man and started selling water.

The prosecutor tried to blame Dirty and Mike for all of the jewelry heists that had occurred over the past months around Cleveland and the judge refused to lower their bonds. They were caught red handed, so they were forced to take a deal. They both copped out to three to fifteen years.

They were granted three visits before they were shipped out. Tonya was the first person to visit Dirty. She brought Tyrone Jr. to see his father before he went to prison. Tonya promised Dirty that she would be by his side during his incarceration.

Next Robin came and seen Dirty, she was too pregnant. She told Dirty that she had moved all of his stuff out of that house and put it in her grandmother's basement. She also told him that his car was parked   in her grandmother's driveway and that once she got her license she would use it to go and visit him. She told him that Dodee was very upset that he did not get to spend one weekend with him as he had promised him.

The last visit that Dirty got was a shock to him. Hobo's mother Mary came to visit him. She told Dirty that she was really sorry that things had turned out the way that they did for him. She told him that she would like to keep in touch with him if he did not mind.

After that visit Dirty went back to his pod. He was awaken early the next morning and transported to Mansfield prison. When he got there he was processed in, then sent to a cell block and put into a cell, which already had a person in it.

They introduced themselves. Then Dirty's celly asked him, "So what are you in for?"

Dirty replied, "Hittin' licks!"

He made his bunk, climbed up on it and laid down. He folded his arms behind his head and laid there staring at the ceiling. He laid there plotting the first lick that he was going to hit when he get out.

New Flavor Books & Publishing LLC
Book Order form

Full Name: _____

Institution# (If applicable):_____

Address: _____

Address 2: _____

City:_____ State:_____ Zip:_____

Book Title:	Price/Quantity
Hood to Hood: A Cleveland Story	$15.00 _____
Hood to Hood 2: Spank's Revenge	$15.00 _____
Sexual Addiction: Director's cut	$15.00 _____
All Flavors A book of Erotic Short Stories	$9.99 _____
Bisexual Bliss	$15.00 _____
Murder or Justice	$15.00 _____
Hittin' Licks	$15.00 _____
Deadly Surgeon	$15.00 _____

Total Including ($3.00) Shipping and Handling _____

To place an order for one of our books please send a payment for the price of the book plus $3.00 for shipping and handling to:

New Flavor Books & Publishing LLC

C/O Book orders

PO Box 603323

Cleveland, Ohio 44103

Please allow 2 - 4 weeks